PENGUIN BOOKS

Kevin Brooks was born in Exeter, Devon, and he studied in Birmingham and London. He has worked in a crematorium, a zoo, a garage and a post office, before – happily – giving it all up to write books. Kevin is the award-winning author of eight novels and lives in North Yorkshire.

'Kevin Brooks just gets better and better, and given that he started off brilliant, that leaves one scratching around for superlatives' – *Sunday Telegraph*

'He's an original. And he writes one hell of a story' – Meg Rosoff, author of *How I Live Now*

'A masterly writer' – *Mail on Sunday*

Westbooks $14.65

Books by Kevin Brooks

BEING
BLACK RABBIT SUMMER
CANDY
KILLING GOD
KISSING THE RAIN
LUCAS
MARTYN PIG
THE ROAD OF THE DEAD

Kevin

Killing

GOD

BROOKS

PENGUIN BOOKS

PENGUIN BOOKS

Published by the Penguin Group
Penguin Books Ltd, 80 Strand, London WC2R 0RL, England
Penguin Group (USA) Inc., 375 Hudson Street, New York, New York 10014, USA
Penguin Group (Canada), 90 Eglinton Avenue East, Suite 700, Toronto, Ontario, Canada M4P 2Y3
(a division of Pearson Penguin Canada Inc.)
Penguin Ireland, 25 St Stephen's Green, Dublin 2, Ireland (a division of Penguin Books Ltd)
Penguin Group (Australia), 250 Camberwell Road, Camberwell, Victoria 3124, Australia
(a division of Pearson Australia Group Pty Ltd)
Penguin Books India Pvt Ltd, 11 Community Centre, Panchsheel Park, New Delhi – 110 017, India
Penguin Group (NZ), 67 Apollo Drive, Rosedale, North Shore 0632, New Zealand
(a division of Pearson New Zealand Ltd)
Penguin Books (South Africa) (Pty) Ltd, 24 Sturdee Avenue, Rosebank, Johannesburg 2196, South Africa

Penguin Books Ltd, Registered Offices: 80 Strand, London WC2R 0RL, England

penguin.com

First published 2009
1

Text copyright © Kevin Brooks, 2009
Grateful acknowledgement is made for permission to include excerpts from the following copyrighted
material: 'About You' words and music by Jim & William Reid copyright © Domino Publishing Company
Limited, 1987; 'Darklands' words and music by Jim & William Reid copyright © Domino Publishing
Company Limited, 1987; 'Head' words and music by Jim & William Reid copyright © Domino Publishing
Company Limited, 1985; 'Her Way of Praying' words and music by William Reid and James Reid
copyright © Domino Publishing Company Limited, 1989; 'Inside Me' words and music by Jim & William
Reid copyright © Domino Publishing Company Limited, 1985; 'Nine Million Rainy Days' words
and music by Jim & William Reid copyright © Domino Publishing Company Limited, 1987.
All rights reserved

The moral right of the author has been asserted

Set in Sabon 11/15pt by Palimpsest Book Production Limited,
Grangemouth, Stirlingshire
Made and printed in England by Clays Ltd, St Ives plc

British Library Cataloguing in Publication Data
A CIP catalogue record for this book is available from the British Library

ISBN: 978-0-141-31912-4

www.greenpenguin.co.uk

inside me (1)

This is a story about me, that's all.

> (*i take my time away*
> *and i see something*
> *and that's my story)*

This is me.

head on

OK, first thing – my name is Dawn Bundy.

Second thing – I'm fifteen years (and seven days) old.

Third thing – I live with my mum in an ordinary house on an ordinary street in an ordinary town in England.

Fourth thing – I'm totally unattractive and I don't give a shit.

Fifth thing – I also tend to exaggerate sometimes, and this is probably one of those times. Which probably means that I *am* unattractive, but I'm not *totally* unattractive (i.e. I'm not eye-burstingly hideous or anything). I'm just kind of non-delectable, if you know what I mean. I have no discernible shape. No womanly, curvy, magazine-girly shape. Basically, I'm just kind of round and plain and lumpyish. So, yes, of course, I *do* give a shit that I'm not delectable. I'd *love* to be delectable – Little Miss Pretty, Little Miss Hot, Little Miss Look-At-Me-And-I'll-Make-You-Quiver. Who *wouldn't* want to be like that? I mean, beauty *isn't* just skin deep, is it? Beauty (and non-beauty) is belly deep, heart deep . . . it's life-de*fin*ingly deep.

Anyway, all I'm trying to say is that I know I'm not beautiful, and that's all there is to it.

Sixth thing – my mum's name is Sara and she's forty-nine years old.

Seventh thing – my dad's name is John and he disappeared two years ago.

And last thing – today is the first day of January, the start of a brand-new year. And tomorrow I'm going to start killing God.

my little underground

It doesn't mean anything, OK? Killing God – it doesn't mean anything. It's just a thing, that's all. Just an idea, something to do, something to keep me occupied. (And, no, it's not a New Year's Resolution either.) I just like doing things that keep my mind off the things I don't want to think about (or, to be more specific, the *thing* I don't want to think about). Last year, for example, towards the end of summer, I did this thing with painted snails. What it was, I was out in the back garden one night, picking up some dog poos (I'll tell you about my dogs later on), and it'd been raining all day, so everything was all wet and horrible, and I happened to notice that the garden path was covered in snails. There were loads of them – all sliming around on the rain-soaked concrete, snailing here and snailing there ... and it got me thinking. I had no idea what I was thinking about, but I didn't really mind. I was happy enough just standing there in the rainy summer night, with a dog-poo bag in my hand, watching the slow-motion dance of the snails, just thinking, thinking, thinking ... thinking about nothing in particular.

And then it hit me.

Letters.

Letters, words, messages.

Snail communication.

What would happen, I wondered, if I collected a load of snails, painted letters on their shells, and then released them back into the garden? I mean, what would I find when I went out into the garden the next night? Would the snails *know* they had letters on their backs? Would they arrange themselves so that the letters spelled out snaily messages to me? HULLO DAWN. WE LUV U (I imagine that snails are very poor spellers). Or maybe the painted snails would slope off into the gardens next door and spell out messages to my neighbours. U BAD. WE KIL U.

And so, with that in mind (and smiling to myself), I dropped the dog-poo bag into the bin, called my dogs, and went back inside to start working it all out. It didn't take long. All I needed was some fluorescent paint, a fine paintbrush, a cardboard box and some snails. The only tricky bit was trying to decide how many letters I should use to make it work – i.e. how many As, how many Bs, how many Cs, and so on. Like in Scrabble, you know? I mean, you don't just have equal numbers of every letter, do you? Because some letters get used a lot more than others. Anyway, after a lot of thinking, and a lot of counting up letters in books and stuff, I eventually realized (kind of dumbly) that it *was* just like Scrabble, so why not just copy the Scrabble letters (i.e. twelve Es, nine As, nine Is, 8 Ns, etc.)? So that's what I did. (Except there are one hundred letters in a Scrabble set, which would have meant collecting one hundred snails. Which is a lot of snails. So I just more or less halved the Scrabble numbers instead.)

Over the next two nights, I collected about fifty snails and painted fluorescent letters on their shells (which took me most of another night), and then I released them all back into the garden. And, yes, I know this all *sounds* pretty dull, but it was actually quite exciting – waiting for the next night to come round, wondering what was going to happen when I went out into the garden with my torch, wondering if the snails had anything to say . . .

Unfortunately, nothing much happened at all.

And the reason that nothing much happened at all was mainly that the fluorescent paint I'd used turned out to be poisonous (*Harmful if swallowed, inhaled, etc. May be fatal to aquatic organisms*). I have no idea how the poisonousness got through the snails' shells into the snails themselves, but it did. And the end result of my snail-communication experiment was:

a) four dead snails, their (still intact) shells spelling out –
MNEH

b) twelve dead snails, their slimily crushed shells unreadable

c) thirty-four missing/presumed dead snails

and d) two dead thrushes.

Q. What's all this got to do with anything?
A. Nothing.

Like I said, I'm just trying to explain the kinds of things I do, that's all. The kinds of things I've been doing for the past two years to keep my mind off the other Dawn, the thirteen-year-old Dawn . . . the Dawn who lives in a cave inside my head. (The cave is small and cold and it has no sound and I try to make it soft like a pillow but most of the time it's hard like stone. It has to be hard to keep out the monsters.)

Anyway, it's tomorrow now, and at this very moment I'm walking along through the covered walkways of the shopping precinct on my way to Waterstone's. (Some of the kids at school call the precinct 'the mall', like it's some kind of really cool place in Beverly Hills or somewhere. But it's not a mall, it's just a tunnel full of shops.) And here I am, walking along through the crowded walkways, with my head bowed down, my eyes fixed to the ground, my hands in my pockets, my dogs trotting along at my feet, and my iPod turned up loud enough to drown out the town-sound of passing voices and drifting muzak and hundreds and hundreds of shuffling feet . . .

And no one can see me, no one at all.

I'm completely invisible.

You know why? I'll tell you why. Because I'm wearing my Invisible Coat, that's why. And that's also why the bookshop's probably going to be closed when I get there. Because if there's one thing that's *guaranteed* to make you late for something, it's trying to find your Invisible Coat before you go out. I spent almost an hour looking for mine this afternoon. I *thought* I'd found it after about fifteen minutes, and it wasn't until I'd put it on and said goodbye to Mum and was halfway down the street that I realized I'd made a mistake. It wasn't my Invisible Coat after all – it was my Nothing Coat.

Mind you, it's an easy mistake to make.

They're both coats, they're both invisible.

The only real difference is that the invisibility of the Nothing Coat is entirely due to its not being there.

This is all crap, of course. I don't have an Invisible Coat. Invisible Coats don't exist. I *do* have a Nothing Coat, but that goes without saying. Everyone has a Nothing Coat. More than one, in fact. You can have as many Nothing Coats as you like – millions, billions, infinitillions – because not only is everything in the world that *isn't* a coat a Nothing Coat, but so is everything in the world that isn't *any*thing.

And that's a lot of things.

I have to shut up now. It's nearly four o'clock, and it's the second of January, which is probably some kind of Day-After-New-Year's-Day holiday or something, which means the shops probably close at four o'clock like they do on Bank Holidays and Sundays . . .

Q. Why do shops close at four o'clock on a Sunday?
A. God knows.

I don't know much about God. I mean, I know all the basic stuff, the kind of stuff they teach you in Religious Studies . . . although, to be honest, I've never paid that much attention in Religious Studies. But I know the kind of stuff that everyone knows – the Bible stories, the miracles, the whole idea of God and the Devil and Jesus and faith and heaven and hell and angels and everything. It's impossible *not* to know about that kind of stuff. It's everywhere – at school, on TV, in books and films and newspapers, in magazines and on CDs, on the streets, on posters, on those signs outside churches that (inexplicably) advertise God (e.g. *WHEN WAS THE LAST TIME YOU TOLD GOD YOU LOVED HIM?* or *TODAY IS A GIFT FROM GOD*) . . . it's everywhere. You can't get away from it. So, yes, I know about all that kind of stuff, but I don't really know much else. You know, like what's the difference between Protestants and Catholics and Presbyterians and Methodists and Anglicans and Baptists and Quakers and Unitarians and Mormons and Jehovah's Witnesses and all the other brands of Christianity? Are they all about the same God? Or do different brands worship different Gods? Or maybe it's all about the same God, but with slightly different packaging – a bit like the packets of cereal you get in supermarkets. You know, like there's the *real* Kellogg's Corn Flakes, but you can also get Tesco Cornflakes, Honey Corn Flakes, Tesco Value Cornflakes, Golden Flakes, Organic Cornflakes . . . and they're all pretty much the same – i.e. they're all kind of corny and flakey, and they're all sold in boxes – but each brand tastes ever so slightly different, and each one is sold in a slightly different box.

I don't know . . .

Maybe it's nothing like that at all.

Not that it makes any difference, of course. Because, unlike Corn Flakes, there is no God. He doesn't exist. Which is why it's going to be kind of difficult to kill him.

i love rock 'n' roll

I'm in Waterstone's now, standing in front of the Bible section. I've got 'I Love Rock 'n' Roll' playing on my iPod, and it's raining outside (Waterstone's is in a little back street just outside the precinct), and it's almost dark, so I'm trying to be as quick as possible, because they don't let dogs in here, so I've had to leave mine outside, and they don't like the rain. Their names, by the way, are Jesus and Mary. And I promised I'd tell you about them later on, and I guess it's later on now. So here goes.

They're dachshunds. More specifically, they're smooth-haired black-and-tan dachshunds. Brother and sister, they're three years old, and I've had them since they were puppies. My dad gave them to me when I was twelve. I'm not sure where he got them from, but I think they were probably a bit too young to be separated from their mother, because they were both really clingy and insecure when I got them, and I suppose I became their surrogate mother. Which is why we've always been really close. We go just about everywhere together. We sleep together, we go shopping together, we watch TV together. The only time we can't be together is when I'm at school. Which is one of the reasons I really hate going to school.

Q. Why are they called Jesus and Mary?
A. Well, actually, there are two answers to this one. The one I usually give is that I named them after my favourite band – The Jesus and Mary Chain. Although 'favourite' is probably the wrong word here. Because, as far as I'm concerned, The Jesus and Mary Chain are The *Only* Band In The World, The Best Band In The Universe, The Only Music Worth Listening To. Their songs are so dark and beautiful, so raw, so pure . . . it's the kind of music that makes you feel like you're sinking down into a big black nowhere.

And I like that.

I first heard them about four years ago when my dad brought home a CD called *Darklands*. He adored it, and for weeks and weeks it was the only thing he played, and the more he played it, the more I fell in love with it. And ever since then, The Jesus and Mary Chain have been THE only band for me. I've downloaded every song they've ever recorded, *and* I've got all their CDs – they're all I ever listen to – and I listen to them all the time. At home, on my PC, on my iPod, whenever and wherever . . . I listen to them so much that even when I'm not listening to them I'm hearing their songs in my head. Their music is the soundtrack to my life. Right now, for example, I've got 'I Love Rock 'n' Roll' on repeat (I play everything on repeat, usually for at least three or four times), and I'll probably keep listening to it until I get home.

So when people ask me why my dogs are called Jesus

and Mary, that's what I tell them – they're named after my favourite band. And it's true. But it's also true that when I first got Jesus and Mary, we had some Christians living next door to us called Mr and Mrs Garth (I knew they were Christians because they had an *I* ❤ *JESUS* sticker in the back of their car), and they were really horrible people. I mean, they used to treat us like we were nothing, like we didn't exist, we were invisible, you know? We'd try being friendly with them, but they just didn't want to know. They'd simply ignore us. For no reason at all. And that really annoyed me. So I called my dogs Jesus and Mary because I knew it would annoy *them*. And it did. Especially at night, when it was nice and quiet, and I'd let my dogs out for a wee, and then I'd have to stand at the back door whistling and calling them in – *JESUS! MARY! C'MON, JESUS! HURRY UP!* Nope, Mr and Mrs Garth didn't like that at all. And they liked it even less when I started calling out *Jeb*us instead of Jesus (I got the idea from an episode of *The Simpsons*). *JEEEBUS! HEY, JEEEB-USS!* For some reason, that *really* bothered the Garths. In fact, it bothered them so much that one night Mr Garth threw open his window and started yelling at me.

'How *dare* you!' he shouted (wimpishly). 'How dare you take Our Lord's name in vain!'

'Sorry?' I said, looking innocently at him.

'You're *despicable*. You really are. You stupid, pitiful little girl.'

Mr and Mrs Garth have moved now.

Thank God.

Have you seen how many Bibles there are in Waterstone's? There's shelves and shelves of them, and they all have different names and different covers. Right now, for example, I can see the *New King James Bible*, the *Authorized King James Bible*, the *New International Bible*, the *Holy Bible: Catholic Edition*, the *Youth Bible* . . . there's even something called the *Good News Bible*. I mean, come on . . . I've got two wet dogs waiting outside – I don't have time for all this.

In the end, I choose one called *Holy Bible: The New Revised Standard Version, With Apocrypha*. It's got the world-famous *Nelson's Unique Fan-Tab™ Index Reference System* (which, apparently, *Helps you find the books of the Bible in an instant!*). It's also got:

- Informative Section Introductions with Line Drawings and Maps
- Topical Subject Headings with Cross-Reference for Further Study
- Self-Pronouncing Text for Ease in Reading
- Textual and Explanatory Footnotes for Enhanced Understanding

and all for only £11.99.

It's a pretty hefty book (1,191 very thin pages), and it looks like it's got at least twenty billion very small words in it, so before I go to the pay desk I nip into the Children's section and get myself a much more accessible-looking *Children's Illustrated Bible* (£9.99).

I remove my earphones, take the Bibles up to the pay desk, and give them to the goateed bookseller guy.

He looks at them, turns them over, scans them with his barcode thing.

'Yeah, that's £21.98, please,' he says.

I dig in my pocket for some money, trying to separate a single £50 note from the rest of the notes I've got stuffed in there, but as I pull it out, the other notes come flopping out with it, and I drop the lot on the counter. There's a fair amount of cash there (which I'll explain in a while) – about £250 or so – and I can see the bookseller guy staring at it, and I can see him wondering what someone like me – i.e. a lumpyish and obviously not very rich fifteen-year-old girl – is doing with so much money.

I don't say anything to him, I just scoop up the notes, pass him the fifty, and jam the rest in my pocket. He hesitates for a moment, then he shrugs (like, who cares?), takes the fifty, holds it up to the light to make sure it's real, puts it in the till, puts the Bibles in a carrier bag, and gives me my change. I gaze at the notes and coins in my hand, momentarily tempted to pick out a £1 coin, hold it up to the light, and squint at it like the bookseller guy just squinted at my fifty, like I'm checking to make sure *it's* real . . . you know, just for a laugh. But I don't suppose he'd find it very funny, and I can't be bothered anyway.

'Do you want your receipt in the bag?' he says.

I nod.

He puts the receipt in the bag and passes it over.

'What time do you close?' I ask him.

'Eight o'clock,' he says, looking at his watch.

'I thought you closed at four?'

'No,' he says. 'Eight o'clock.'

'What time do you close on Sundays?'

'Yeah, four o'clock on a Sunday.'

'Why's that?'

He gives me an impatient look. 'What?'

'Why do you close at four on Sundays?'

He shrugs again. 'I don't know ... we just do.'

I thank him, pick up my Bibles, go outside, collect Jesus and Mary, and head off into the winter-dark rain.

happy when it rains (1)

This rain is the kind of rain that shivers like silver in the dark. It soaks into everything, like a fine spray of mist, and it seeps right into you, all the way down to your bones. And I'd *like* to like it. I'd like to be happy when it rains – in a darkly romantic/Jesus and Mary Chain kind of way – but I don't. It's just cold and wet and horrible. Jesus and Mary don't like it either. And as I'm scuttling back down the street towards the shelter of the shopping precinct, they keep stopping every few steps or so to shake themselves. I don't know why they bother, because they've never been the best shakers in the world. Their legs are too short, for a start. I mean, it's hard to shake with any real vigour when your legs are no bigger than a fat man's finger. And even if they *could* shake themselves effectively, they don't really have any hair to shake. So, all in all, it's a fairly pointless exercise. But they do it anyway. Waddle, waddle . . . shake, shake . . . waddle, waddle . . . shake, shake . . .

'Come on,' I keep telling them. 'Hurry up. I haven't got all day.'

Which is a lie, of course.

I've got *more* than all day. I've got all day, all evening, all night, all of the next day...

I don't really have any human friends. My only real friends are Jesus and Mary. And they're dogs. Of course, I'm not saying that I don't *know* any humans, because I do. I know most of the kids in my year at school, and quite a few who aren't in my year, and some of the kids who live down my street. I know their names, and what they look like, and what kind of people they are... and sometimes I even talk to some of them. But they're not what I'd call friends.

I suppose most people think of me as a loser. And they're probably right. But it doesn't bother me. I mean, yes, OK, I *am* a loser – but I'm a perfectly content kind of loser. I don't *want* to be in with the in-crowd, and I genuinely don't care what anyone thinks or says about me. And, yes, because of that (and also because I'm smarter than your average bear), I get a few dirty looks now and then, and some of the other kids sometimes try to get me going by calling me names. *Lesbian* seems to be the most popular one. Although, come to think of it, I don't get called a lesbian as much as I used to. In fact, I haven't been called a lesbian for ages. Which could mean that the name-callers have realized that I really don't care what they call me, or it could just mean that lesbians are kind of cool these days, so calling me a lesbian simply doesn't work as an insult any more.

Anyway, the long and short of it is – I don't fit in, and I don't *want* to fit in, so most of the time everyone pretty much leaves me alone.

Which is why, as I'm nearing the entrance to the precinct, I'm surprised to see Mel Monroe and Taylor Harding, the two bad-assiest girls from school, coming out of Accessorize and looking at me with some kind of *interest*.

I don't stop walking, of course.

I just keep my head down and keep going. Keep going, keep going, keep listening to the music, keep pretending that I don't hear Mel and Taylor shouting out behind me: 'Dawn! Hey, Dawn! Hold on a minute. DAWN!'

But you can only pretend to ignore so much, can't you? And when Mel and Taylor suddenly appear on the pavement right in front of me, jumping around and waving their hands to get my iPodded attention, I don't really have much choice, do I? I have to stop, looking at them with feigned surprise. I have to turn off my iPod and pull out my earphones and listen to what they're saying.

'Hey, Dawn,' Taylor is saying. 'Where're you going? Where've you been?'

She's all lipsticked up, her eyes black and lashy, and despite the cold and the rain, all she's wearing is a short denim skirt and a bright-white puffy little jacket.

'Uh ... I'm not going anywhere,' I mutter. 'I'm just ... you know ...'

'Y'all right?' says Mel.

I look at her, wondering what the hell's going on. Why are these two talking to me? They *never* talk to me. They wouldn't be seen dead talking to me, *especially* outside Accessorize, with a bunch of their bad-assy friends still hanging around inside, and with me in my Nothing Coat and my baggy black trousers and my worn-out old boots, clutching a bag full of Bibles. But here they are, asking me where I'm going, if I'm all right...

'Yeah,' I tell Mel. 'Yeah, I'm all right.'

She nods her head, chewing gum. She's shorter than Taylor, and prettier too... in a cheap kind of way. But cheap looks good on her. And she knows it.

'They yours?' Taylor asks me, looking down at Jesus and Mary, who are both sitting patiently at my feet.

'Yeah,' I say.

'They bite?'

'Only if I tell them to.'

'What kind of dogs are they?'

'Dachshunds.'

'What hoonds?'

'Dachshunds.'

'Sausage dogs,' Mel explains.

Taylor nods, not really interested. She glances at the carrier bag in my hand. 'What've you got in there?'

I shrug. 'Just some books.'

'Books?' (Like I've just told her I've got a couple of turds in the bag.) 'What kind of books?'

I shrug again. 'Just books, you know...'

'Right.' She looks over her shoulder, staring at a couple of girls coming out of Accessorize, then she turns back to me. 'What're you doing tonight?'

'What?'

'Tonight... what are you doing?'

'Why?'

'D'you want to come to a party?'

'A party?'

19

She sighs. 'Are you deaf?'

Mel laughs.

I look at her.

'We're having a little party, that's all,' she tells me, flicking her hair. 'Just a few people, you know. Music. A few drinks. D'you want to come?'

I almost say, 'Do *I* want to come?' but I manage to stop myself just in time. My face still says it though: *A party? You're having a little party and you want* me *to come?*

'You all right?' Mel says, frowning at me.

'Yeah . . . yeah, sorry. I was just –'

'Look,' Taylor says hurriedly, glancing over her shoulder again, 'we've got to get going, OK?'

'Right . . .'

She leans towards me. 'So?'

'What?'

Another sigh. 'So . . . do you want to come to this party or not?'

'Umm, I don't know . . . where is it?'

Mel and Taylor answer me at the same time: 'My place.'

'Sorry?'

They look at each other for a moment, both of them slightly annoyed (but trying not to show it), then they turn back to me, suddenly all smiles again.

'It's at *my* place,' Taylor says. 'It was going to be at Mel's, but . . . uhh . . .'

'My mum's going to be there,' Mel continues. 'I thought she was going out, you know, but she changed her mind. So we're having the party at Taylor's instead.'

'Right,' I say. 'And her mum's *not* going to be there?'

'No,' says Taylor. 'So, you know, if you want to come along, have some fun . . .' She winks at me. 'It's Nelson Lane, across from the park. You know where that is?'

'Yeah.'

'Number 57,' she says. 'Nine o'clock.'

'Right.'

And that's just about it. They turn round and walk away up the street, giggling and whispering to each other, waggling their backsides, and Taylor says something to Mel, and Mel slaps her playfully on the arm, and Taylor lets out an ugly shriek of laughter . . . and I'm left standing here on the pavement, cold and wet and confused.

I look down at Jesus and Mary.

'Any idea what that was all about?' I ask them.

Mary yawns.

Jesus licks his arse.

'Yeah, thanks,' I say. 'That's really helpful.'

inside me (2)

I'm on the bus on the way home now. Rainwater is dripping from coats and umbrellas, and I can smell the sour scent of rainwet clothes and old people. I'm sitting upstairs, near the back, with Jesus and Mary lying on the floor at my feet. Mary is shivering.

'It's all right,' I tell her, scratching her head. 'We'll be home soon.'

how soon?

'Soon.'

I should have brought their coats. If I'd brought their coats, they wouldn't have got so cold and wet.

I'm an idiot.

I turn on my iPod, scroll through the menu, and select 'Inside Me'. A moment's silence, a tick of a drum, then the bass comes in and the guitars start buzzing and

> *(i take my time away
> and i see something)*

I see too much.

In the thick glass windows, I see the colourless reflections of other passengers. I see a small boy resting his chin on the silver rail of a seat-back, grinning at the buzz of the bus vibrating through his head. His mother hisses loudly at him – '*Dennis!*' – and when he ignores her, she yanks his arm with a charmless hand and hisses even louder, '*I won't tell you again!*'

Dennis doesn't care.

Further down the bus, I see a twenty-something man, all dirty fingernails and pock-marked skin, flapping the pages of a computer magazine, looking – I imagine – for something he wants. In front of him, two thin teenage girls in tight clothes are whispering to each other, exchanging smirks and stifled snorts, and in front of them a young boy about my age sits alone, toying uncomfortably with the drawstring of his coat hood.

On the back of the seat in front of me there's a graffitied swastika, a toothy head, and something that looks like a giant hairy amoeba. I don't think it's *supposed* to be a giant hairy amoeba, but that's what it looks like. On the floor, there's a couple of lumps of chewing gum and a piece of cellophane.

The town passes by in the silver-black rain. Streets, roads, street-trees, empty playing fields, orange lights, power lines, a thousand houses, cars and people. The green-grey slick of the river. A bridge. A row of small estate shops . . . where, beneath the awning of a newsagent's, a sad-looking girl is reading the postcard messages stuck in the shop window . . . but I don't think she's really reading them. I think she's just waiting for someone. And I wonder for a moment who she's waiting for – her boyfriend, her mother, her father?

The sad-looking girl is looking away from the window now, dragging a lock of hair behind her ear, and as she peers hopefully down the street, the shop door opens and an Asian man comes out, crouches down beside her, and padlocks a big chain to the bubblegum machine.

(I can see all these things from inside my cave but it's too small and dark in here for anyone or anything to see me.)

In the seat behind me, an old man hacks up an old-man's cough – *kah*!

(My name is Dawn.
  I'm thirteen years old.
  My name is Dawn.)

I close my cave eyes and open my carrier bag and get out my Holy Bible.

(i've seen it all before)

I already know how the Bible begins (*In the beginning*, etc.) so instead of starting at the first page, I just kind of open it up and flip through the flappy-thin pages and start reading something at random. And the first thing I come across (and I'm not kidding you here, this really is the straight-up truth) . . . the first thing I come across is a really weird story about a Levite and his concubine. Of course, I have no idea what a Levite or a concubine is, but according to the *Textual and Explanatory Footnotes for Enhanced Understanding*, at the back of the Bible, a Levite is: "a descendant of *Levi*: an inferior priest of the ancient Jewish Church: (also without *cap.*) a clergyman (*slang*). And a concubine is not (as I thought) some kind of biblical porcupine, it's: °one (esp. a woman) who cohabits without being married: a mistress. OK, so it's a story about some kind of old priest and his girlfriend or mistress, and I think they're just travelling around Israel or something, and they're in this place called Gibeah, and for some reason they can't find anywhere to stay. Then this old man comes along and tells them they can stay at his place if they want, and so they all go off to this old man's house and everything's cool for a while – he feeds their donkeys, makes them dinner, gives them something to drink.

But then this happens:

22While they were enjoying themselves, the men of the city, a perverse lot, surrounded the house, and started pounding on the door. They said to the old man, the master of the house, "Bring out the man who came into your house, so that we may have intercourse with him." **23**And the man, the master of the house, went out to them and said to them, "No, my brothers, do not act so wickedly. Since this man is my guest, do not do this vile thing. **24**Here are my virgin daughter and his concubine; let me bring them out now. Ravish them and do whatever you want to them; but against this man do not do such a vile thing." **25**But the men would not listen to him. So the man seized his concubine and put her out to them. They wantonly raped her, and abused her all through night until the morning. And as the dawn began to break, they let her go. **26**As morning appeared, the woman came and fell down at the door of the man's house where her master was, until it was light. **27**In the morning her master got up, opened the doors of the house, and when he went out to go on his way, there was his concubine lying at the door of the house with her hands on the threshold. **28**"Get up," he said to her, "we are going." But there was no answer. Then he put her on the donkey; and the man set out for his home. **29**When he had entered his house, he took a knife, and grasping his concubine he cut her into twelve pieces, limb by limb, and sent her throughout the territory of Israel.

And that's it. Honestly. You can check it out if you want – it's chapter 19 in the book of Judges. That's the story. A bunch of tough guys (who've obviously been down the pub) want to have sex with the priest, but the old man won't let them because the priest is his guest, and of course it's *really* bad manners to allow your male guest to be gang-raped. So what the old man does, he tells this gang of drunken perverts that they can't have the priest, but they're more than welcome to ravish his virgin daughter and the priest's girlfriend instead. For some reason, though, this alternative offer doesn't seem to interest the gang all that much, so the priest just grabs his girlfriend and chucks her out of the house, and the men outside spend all night wantonly raping her and abusing her. And then, in the morning, when the priest opens the door and finds this poor girl lying on the doorstep, he just kind of looks at her and says, 'Get up. We're going.' But she's dead. So he takes her back home and cuts her up into twelve pieces.

Which is fair enough, I suppose.

I mean, what else are you going to do with a dead concubine?

I close the Bible then, not sure I want to read any more. Of course, this horror story is probably some kind of allegory or something, one of those things that's not meant to be taken literally. I mean, it's probably not as sick as it sounds.

But still . . .

It kind of stinks, doesn't it?

cut dead

I'm half thinking of God and half thinking of Taylor and Mel as I get off the bus at the end of Whipton Lane. The street lights are on, dazzling orange in the still-falling rain, and the night's getting colder. I keep my head down and hurry along Whipton Lane, then right, into Dane Street. My street. This is where I live.

It's a nothing place, really, the same as every other nothing place in the world. Terraced houses, brick walls, a too-narrow street full of too many parked cars. The usual selection of discarded crap is slopping around in the rain-streamed gutters – empty carrier bags and crisp packets, disintegrating cigarette ends and dog shit – and halfway down the street there's a miniature lake of dirty grey water where the drain has blocked up again.

It's not exactly paradise.

But, then again, it's hardly hell either.

Jesus and Mary know where we are now, they can smell the smell of home. And they've both started trotting along in front of me, going as fast as they can without actually running, desperate to get out of the cold and rain. Home is warm, home is dry, home is food. That's what they're thinking.

Mel Monroe, I'm half thinking.

Mel Monroe.

Mel is the bad girl who all the other bad girls look up to. She's hard and she's hot. She doesn't take any shit. She knows what's what. Mel Monroe can ruin your life just by looking at you the wrong way. And until about six months ago, she was The One, The Only One, and no one else was anywhere near her. But then Taylor Harding showed up, expelled (it was rumoured) from a school on the other side of town. Expelled (it was variously rumoured) for fighting, for drinking, for taking drugs, for having sex with a boy in the gymnasium, for having sex with a *girl* in the gymnasium, for carrying a knife, a gun . . . a bazooka. Whatever. You know what rumours are like. Anyway, when she first showed up at school – with her big bad blonde reputation – it was generally assumed that there was bound to be some kind of showdown between her and Mel eventually. But, surprisingly, it never came. The two of them spent the first couple of days kind of circling around each other, eyeing each other up, getting the measure of each other, but then, on the third morning, to everyone's astonishment, they turned up at school together walking arm in arm. It was as if they'd been best-bosom-buddies for ever – walking the walk together, looking the look . . . and all at once Mel wasn't The Only One any more. Mel and *Taylor* were The Only One. The Only Two. MelandTaylor. Joined at the hip, like some kind of bad-ass Siamese twins.

But none of this had anything to do with me. Not then, and not now. Yes, I know what's going on at school. And, yes, I hear things and I see things, and I know what's what and who's who . . . but no one can see me, remember? I'm invisible. *Nothing* has anything to do with me.

So why, I'm half thinking now, why would Mel and Taylor ask *me* to come to a party? Why would *any*one ask me to come to a party?

Meanwhile, the other half of me (the half that isn't thinking about Taylor and Mel) is thinking about killing God.

Killing God?

Why?

How?

What does it even mean?

And then I see Splodge, sitting on his doorstep in the rain.

His real name is Steven Lodge. He's younger than me – maybe ten or eleven – and I don't really know him that well, but his house is only four doors down from mine, so I see him around quite a lot. He always wears a cheap Primark parka, no matter what the weather, and he's always on his own. Which is kind of why I quite like him. Everyone calls him Splodge (except, I imagine, his parents) because:

(1) His middle name is Peter, which makes him S. P. Lodge (which you would have thought his parents might have realized, but obviously they didn't. Or maybe they did, and they just thought it was funny).

And (2) he has one of those big purpley-red birthmarks on his face. And, unfortunately, it *is* pretty splodge-like. It covers most of the left-hand side of his face, and of course people don't like looking at it, so they don't know where to look when they're talking to him, and they don't know how they're supposed to react to it (ignore it? say something about it?), and that makes them feel really cringey and awkward ... so most people just leave him alone. Like he's diseased or something. So most of the time he just hangs around on his own – sometimes kicking a ball about, sometimes just wandering around, and sometimes (like now) just sitting on his doorstep, watching the world go by.

He smiles now as Jesus and Mary waddle up to him for a quick sniff of his trainers.

'You're wet,' he says to them, scratching Mary's head.

'It's the rain,' I say, stopping beside him and turning off my iPod. 'It usually has that wettening effect on things.'

He looks up at me. 'You ought to get them a coat.'

'They've got coats.'

He smiles at me. His birthmark is really purpley today. It's the cold weather. His splodge gets purpley when it's cold and orangey-red when it's hot.

'All right?' I ask him.

'Yeah.'

'What are you doing?'

'Not much ...' He glances at the carrier bag in my hand. 'Get anything good?'

'Bibles,' I tell him.

'Bibles?'

'Yeah.'

As I wipe a sheen of rain from my forehead, Splodge turns his attention to a passing van. It's a blue one, with *Farthings Furniture* written on the side. It's a cronky old thing, all patched up and rusty, with a bent aerial and a taped-up headlight and windows so dirty you can't see through them. I've seen it around before.

Splodge keeps his eyes on it as it passes by and heads up to the end of Dane Street before turning left into Whipton Lane. Then he turns back to me.

'Do you know who that is?' he asks.

'What – in the van?'

'Yeah . . . I keep seeing it around here all the time. Sometimes it's driving around, sometimes it's parked, but I've never seen anyone get out of it.'

'Maybe it's the FBI,' I suggest. 'Maybe they're spying on you.'

He doesn't smile.

I look at him. 'Can I ask you something?'

He sniffs. 'What?'

'Do you believe in God?'

He frowns at me. 'God?'

'Yeah . . . I mean, do you really think there's some kind of supernatural being that created everything and knows everything and sees everything?'

He shrugs. 'I don't know . . . I've never really thought about it, to be honest.'

'Do you ever go to church?'

'Yeah, sometimes.'

'Do you say prayers and stuff?'

He nods. 'Yeah . . . I say my prayers every night before I go to bed.'

'Really?'

'Yeah.'

'You pray to God?'

'Yeah.'

'But you don't know if you believe in him or not?'

He shrugs again.

'What do you pray for?' I ask him.

'A new face.'

her way of praying (1)

I go into the house the back way (down the alleyway, turn right, turn right) and the dogs run on ahead of me and let themselves into the kitchen through the dog flap in the door. (It's actually a *cat* flap, but they're dogs ... so, you know ... I always think of it as a dog flap.) I follow them into the kitchen, take off my boots and my iPod, then grab a dog towel from the dog cupboard and give Jesus and Mary a good rub down.

'Is that you, Dawn?' Mum calls out from the front room as I'm drying off Jesus's ears.

'Yeah,' I call back. 'Just sorting out the dogs.'

'Are you all right?'

'Yeah. I'll be in in a minute.'

'OK.'

After I've finished drying them off, the dogs get their dinner. Half a beaker of Eukanuba each, topped off with a bit of warm water. I stand and watch them eating. I love the sound they make when they're scoffing their food – the warm-wet chomp of their mouths, the quiet shuffling of their podgy little feet, the faint metal jingling as their dog tags rattle against the rims of the dog bowls ...

I wish I could enjoy things as much as they do.

When they're finished, I give them their afters (a Bonio each) and then I go into the front room. Mum's sitting in her armchair, as ever, watching our huge (52-inch) plasma TV. It's about all she ever does since Dad disappeared – she just sits there, hour after hour, with the remote control and a copy of *TV & Satellite Week* to hand, watching TV.

It's her existence.

That and the drink and the pills.

She picks up the remote now, mutes the TV, then looks round and smiles at me. 'Everything all right, love?'

'Yeah, thanks.' I glance at the TV. On the screen, Jeremy Clarkson is standing next to a bright red sports car, his stupid big hands half stuffed in his stupid jeans pockets. '*Top Gear*?' I ask Mum.

She nods.

'Any good?'

She shrugs. 'It's all right.'

She watches just about anything. Old stuff, new stuff, sci-fi, documentaries, comedies, soaps, films, sport, mysteries, thrillers . . . sometimes I wonder if she actually knows what she's watching. Whatever's on, she just seems to look at it, rather than actually watching it. And her eyes . . . well, her eyes are always kind of not-quite-there, but that's mainly because of the drink.

She drinks a lot, my mum.

In fact, since Dad disappeared, she drinks pretty much all of the time.

(it's her way of talking to jesus)

35

Whisky and coffee is what she drinks. Whisky in black coffee. The whisky keeps her drunk, the coffee keeps her awake. She drinks mugs of it, all day and all night long. And on top of that there's the prescribed antidepressants, and the occasional joint, and the unprescribed sleeping pills (which she has to get off the Internet because her doctor won't give them to her any more). So it's not really surprising that her eyes are kind of glazed most of the time.

But it's OK.

I mean, she's OK.

She functions.

We look after each other.

She's my mum.

We love each other.

'I'd better get some shopping in,' I tell her. 'We're running a bit low.'

She nods, taking a sip from her mug. 'Thanks, love.'

'I'll do it now.'

She smiles. 'I'll make you something to eat. Toasted sandwiches OK?'

'Yeah, perfect.'

Upstairs, in Mum's bedroom, I crouch down beside her bed and fold back the worn red rug (as I've folded it back so many times before), then I hook my finger into the familiar-feeling knothole in the floorboard underneath, and I gently ease it up. I take the £230 (give or take) from my pocket, lean down into the gap under the floorboards, and unzip the dark-green holdall that's been living there for the past two years. I pause for a moment, gazing down through the dusty gloom at the contents of the holdall, and I wonder (as I've wondered so many times before) where it all came from and what it all means... and why and when and where and who ... and then (as always) I just shake my head and try to forget it.

I put the £230 back into the holdall, zip it up, replace the floorboard and the worn red rug, and head off back to my room.

I'm sitting at my desk now, staring dimly at my PC screen as I log on to Tesco's website. Jesus and Mary are settled down in their baskets, and 'Her Way of Praying' is blasting out from my PC speakers

(she's keeping time
keeping time
with the mystery rhyme)

and I'm not wondering where anything came from any more, I'm not asking myself questions, I'm not thinking about Mum... I'm not thinking about anything. I'm just doing what I'm doing – doing the shopping. I usually do it once every two weeks, but what with Christmas and New Year and everything, the schedule's got a bit mixed up. Not that it matters. We always get exactly the same stuff, so all I have to do is log on, sign in, and repeat the last order. I mean, sometimes I'll spend a bit of time browsing the website to see if there's any clothes I want to buy, or maybe some stationery or some computer stuff or something. And sometimes Mum might ask me to get her a book (she only reads books with TV connections, like *CSI* novels or Richard and Judy Book Club picks . . . or occasionally stuff by Jamie Oliver or Trinny and Susannah (although God knows why she reads this stuff, seeing as how she never cooks or cares how she looks)). But mostly it's the same old shopping list every time.

So, anyway, I log on, sign in, select a delivery time, put in the order, pay for it, sign out, log off . . . and by the time I've finished, Mum's brought me up a plate of toasted ham sandwiches and a glass of Coke, and we've talked for a bit (about not very much), and then she's gone back downstairs, back to her armchair and her drink and her TV, and I'm left sitting here on my bed with my dogs and my sandwiches and my Coke and my Bibles.

It's 6.30 p.m.

Of course, I have no intention at all of going to Mel and Taylor's party, but if I *was* thinking of going (which I'm not), I'd have about two hours now to get ready.

But I'm not going, am I?

Why would I?

I bite into a toasted ham sandwich and open up the *Children's Illustrated Bible.*

(hope in hope in the sky)

There's nothing in the *Children's Illustrated Bible* about the Levite and his concubine, which isn't really surprising. I mean, you don't want little kids reading about that kind of stuff, do you? They might get the wrong idea. So, no, there's no raping or ravishing in this good book. All I can find in the place where the Levite/concubine story should be (i.e. in the book of Judges) is some stuff about a guy called Gideon, and a load of other people who're trying to kill him, and the story of Samson and Delilah, which I already know. There are lots of pictures, of course (seeing as how it's an illustrated Bible), but they're not that great, and there are no pictures of God, which is kind of what I'm looking for (because if I know what he looks like, it might make it easier to find him and kill him). Most of the pictures fall into one of two categories:

Category One: pictures of beardy men doing the kinds of things that beardy men do – i.e. standing around talking, leaning on sticks, looking serious about something.

Category Two: pictures of meek-and-virginal-looking women wearing long smocky dresses and hoods, so all you can see is their worshipful faces and their stupid Bambi-like eyes.

But one of the women is different.

And that's Eve.

Eve is very different.

Eve, for some reason, is really sexy.

I mean, obviously, she's naked at the start of the book, so she's bound to look a little bit sexier than the smock-wearing humble women, but it's not just that. (And, besides, it's not as if you can see much of her anyway. Most of her top half is covered up by her luscious blonde hair, and you can't see any of her bottom half because she's standing behind a conveniently placed bush (no visual pun intended, I assume). Adam, by the way, is also naked. And he's also standing behind the bush. Although, oddly enough, in one of the pictures (in which he's *not* standing behind the bush), his naughty bits are covered up by the trailing foot of a chimpanzee that just happens to be nestling in Adam's arms.

A chimpanzee?

What's *that* all about?)

But, no, it's not *just* Eve's nakedness that makes her look sexy, it's the way she's standing there offering Adam an apple, with her pouty red lips and her Kate Moss cheekbones and her come-to-bed eyes. I mean, I know the whole Adam and Eve thing is supposed to be about temptation and stuff, but still . . . I don't know. It just seems a bit unnecessary, that's all. Even on the next page, *after* they've eaten the apple and put on some clothes, Eve's still a lot hotter than all the other Bible girls. Her animal-skin dress is a lot shorter (slit right up to her waist). Her legs are a lot longer (like she's wearing invisible high heels). And (unlike the meek-and-virginal girls) she actually has some cleavage. And she looks like she knows it too.

Q. Why are you so obsessed with these stupid little drawings of Eve?

A. I don't know.

But it makes me wonder – as I've often wondered – if maybe the idiots who used to call me a lesbian weren't quite so idiotic after all.

Q. Are you physically attracted to Eve?

A. I don't know.

Yes, I think she's sexy. But I don't think I'd actually want to *do* anything with her. I just like the way she looks. And, besides, even if I *did* want to do anything with her (which I don't), I wouldn't know where to start.

Q. What about Adam? Do you like the way he looks?
A. No.

But that's simply because he's not very attractive. His arms are too thin. His beard looks false (and ginger). His teeth are like piano keys. All in all, he looks like a slightly deranged rambler.

Q. Are there any boys that you *do* find physically attractive?
A. I haven't come across one yet.

But that doesn't mean I'm a lesbian, does it? It could just mean that I'm not physically attracted to either boys *or* girls ... or that I *am* (attracted to either or both), but I'm too messed up by what happened with Dad to think about my feelings or physically do anything about them.

Q. What happened with Dad?
A. Nothing ... nothing happened.

darklands (1)

There aren't many things I like. I like my mum, my dogs, The Jesus and Mary Chain. I like lying on my bed with my dogs and listening to The Jesus and Mary Chain while my mum's downstairs watching TV (which is what I'm doing right now). I like doing things that keep my mind off the other Dawn. And, as you've probably noticed, I like making lists.

    Q. Why do you like making lists?
    A. Because:
        (a) Listing things makes them easier to understand.
        (b) There is no (b). (I just thought, you know, it'd be kind of neat to make a list of my reasons for liking lists. But I've only got the one reason really, and I'm not sure you can have a list of just one thing. So I added another thing.)

I don't know why a list of things is easier to understand than a non-list of things, but it is. And that's why I need to start listing my reasons for wanting to kill God.
    Why do I want to kill God?
    All right, let's see.

<u>Reason One</u>: If God was dead, there wouldn't be any more Christians. And that would mean there wouldn't be any more door-to-door religion-sellers, those abhorrently offensive people who think they have a right to ring your doorbell and poke their noses into your life and ask you questions about what you think and feel about things.

God, I hate those people.

(And when you get to <u>Reason Three</u>, you'll realize why – and how much – I hate them.)

I *despise* them.

The last time they came to our house, about three weeks before Christmas, they made my mum cry. It was around lunchtime, and I'd taken the day off school because Mum was having one of her really bad days. She gets them sometimes – days when she can't stop thinking about Dad, days when everything gets too much for her . . . she just kind of breaks down a bit. There's not really all that much I can do for her, but I still try to be at home when she gets like that, you know, just in case . . .

So, anyway, that day, when the doorbell rang, I was out in the garden with Jesus and Mary. It'd been snowing, and I was trying to make a snowdog . . . actually, I was trying to make a snow-dachshund, but it's not as easy as it sounds, and I wasn't really having much luck. I had my iPod on, of course, so I didn't hear the doorbell ringing, but I could see that Jesus and Mary had heard something, and from the way they went rushing into the house, yapping and howling like short-legged sausage-wolves, I knew there was someone at the door. But, unfortunately, by the time I got there, Mum had already answered it. And the three Christians in the doorway – two women and one man – were smiling at her and talking at her and ever so kindly pushing leaflets into her hands . . . and she was crying. I mean, she was *crying*. And then I saw one of the smiling Christian women step forward and gently touch Mum on the arm, and I heard this awful smiling woman say something about God and faith and healing, which only made my mum cry even more . . .

And that's when I set the dogs on them.

Reason Two: If God was dead, the shops could stay open later on Sundays.

Reason Three: If God was dead, my dad would never have become addicted to him. And if he'd never become addicted to God, he'd never have lost himself. And if he'd never lost himself . . .

(as sure as life means nothing)

My dad always had a lot of demons in his head. I don't know where they came from, or what they were, all I know (or *think* I know) is that he had stuff inside his head (and his heart) that he didn't want to know, and he spent most of his time trying to forget it was there. And I guess that's why he lived his life the way he did. I mean, don't get me wrong, he was a truly wonderful man, and he loved me and my mum so much, and we loved him, that it makes me cry just thinking about it. He was just such a brilliant dad, you know? He used to take me to places all the time (the park, the cinema, the library, the zoo), and he was always telling me stories, making me laugh, playing me songs, singing to me . . . he even used to dance with me sometimes.

I'll always remember the day, about four or five years ago, when he took Mum and me on a (non-birthday) surprise trip to London. He didn't tell us where we were going or anything, he just woke us up quite early in the morning and told us to hurry up and get dressed because we were all going out for the day. At first, me and Mum just thought he was taking us to the beach or something, but when a taxi arrived and drove us to the train station, and we got there just in time to catch the train to London (on which we had first-class reservations) . . . well, it was pretty obvious then that we weren't just going to the beach. And it became even more obvious when we arrived in London and there was a stretch limousine waiting for us outside the station. I mean, I know that stretch limos aren't that big a deal any more, but it was still pretty cool, and (because we were all so totally *un*cool) it was pretty funny too. Which is why, as we piled into the back of the limousine, we were all smiling and giggling like idiots. Inside, the limo was all decked out with leather seats and luxury gadgets and stuff, and the driver was wearing a uniform and a cap, and as he drove us around London, Mum and Dad helped themselves to posh-looking drinks from posh-looking bottles (and I had some iced Coke in a tall glass), and Dad kept pointing out all the famous landmarks to me (Buckingham Palace, Big Ben, Trafalgar Square) . . . and eventually we pulled up outside this huge swanky hotel, and a hotel guy (who was also wearing a uniform and a cap) opened the car door for us and welcomed us to the hotel . . . and that was really funny too, because he kept kind of bowing his head and calling Mum and Dad *Madam* and *Sir*, and I don't think either of them had ever been treated like that before. Especially not

45

Dad. I mean, my dad was kind of grungy, a bit punky, a little bit hippy-y. I'm sure you know what I mean – shoulder-length dyed-blond hair, black nail varnish, baggy jumpers with holes in them, ripped black jeans, earrings, studs, patchouli oil . . . kind of like a middle-aged (and undead) Kurt Cobain. A Kurt Cobain who wasn't famous and lived with his wife and daughter in a crappy little two-bedroomed house.

So, anyway, despite my dad's non-famous grunginess (and me and Mum's general scruffiness), this hotel guy *Madam*-ed and *Sir*-ed us into the hotel, and Dad (with a sly wink at me) slipped him a £5 tip (God knows where he got the money for all this, by the way . . . although I'm pretty sure now that it must have come from some kind of dodgy-dealery) and then Dad led us into the hotel restaurant, which was un-believably enormous and plush, and we had what was probably the most expensive meal in the world.

It was fantastic.

Mum and Dad couldn't stop smiling at each other all the time.

Dad kept grinning at me.

And I was just sitting there, stuffing my face, looking around (with wide-open eyes) at the rich people eating their dinners.

It was wonderful.

But that was only the start of it.

After we'd eaten ourselves stupid, Dad surprised us again by taking us up to the fifteenth floor and showing us into the best room in the hotel, which he'd not only booked for the night, but he'd also had filled with all kinds of incredibly nice stuff. There were big bunches of flowers all over the place, boxes of chocolates, bottles of champagne, jars of sweets, some stupidly nice stuffed animals, a selection of DVDs and computer games . . . he'd even got hold of a big pile of board games from somewhere – Monopoly, Twister, Cluedo, Risk.

It was like an Aladdin's cave in there.

A very luxurious Aladdin's cave.

We spent the rest of the day out and about in London (in our stretch limousine), shopping and seeing the sights, then we came back to the hotel for a rest, then we went out again, this time to an ice-skating rink (where Dad fell over at least a hundred times), and then, at night, we just stayed in the hotel room playing games and watching TV and ordering room service and dancing like fools to rubbishy old songs and laughing ourselves stupid until we couldn't stay awake any more. And then, finally, some time in the early hours of the morning, we all clambered dozily into a bed the size of a football pitch and fell asleep in each other's arms.

(and heaven i think
is too close to hell)

Yeah, he was the best, my dad. Even when he was at his worst, he really was the best. But, like I said, he had his problems.

(take me to the dark)

I don't really understand a lot of these things, so it's kind of hard to explain them, but I think that one of Dad's problems was that he just didn't want to grow up, because growing up

47

(as far as I know) means facing reality, taking responsibility, being normal. And Dad didn't want any of that. All he ever wanted to do was have fun, listen to music, get drunk, take drugs, forget about the bad stuff, pretend everything was OK . . . and I think Mum was fine with that for a while. She was pretty wild and punky herself, and she was perfectly happy to carry on living it up with Dad, even after I came along. But, as time went on, I think she just got a bit bored with it all. I mean, she didn't stop having fun or listening to music or getting drunk or taking drugs, but she didn't do it *all* the time.

Unlike Dad.

Dad never stopped.

His demons wouldn't let him.

By the time I was around eight or nine, he was already spiralling out of control. Instead of simply *wanting* drugs, he was *needing* drugs. Heroin, mostly. I mean, he'd take anything and everything given the chance, but it was heroin that he was addicted to. And then he started dealing to feed his addiction, and that got him mixed up with all the wrong people, and that led to him getting busted a couple of times and spending a few months in prison. And that kind of scared him into realizing what he was doing, and eventually he managed to kick his heroin habit. But instead of staying clean, he just started drinking like a madman, and for the next few years my truly wonderful dad became this truly horrendous puffy-faced alcoholic.

And then, one day . . .

Mum and me had been out shopping together (well, not so much *shopping* together as walking around town together, looking in shop windows at stuff we'd like to buy if we had any money), and Mum was in a fairly bad mood about something, which I guessed was something to do with Dad, because the day before I'd heard them shouting at each other, and later that night I'd heard her crying quietly in their bedroom.

Anyway, it must have been about four o'clock when we got back from town. The November sky was already darkening, and a cold drizzly rain was beginning to fall. After we'd hurried back home from the bus stop and let ourselves into the comparative warmth of the house, the first thing I noticed was the whiffy smell of dog poo. Jesus and Mary were about seven or eight months old at the time, and although they were pretty much house-trained, they still had their little accidents now and then – especially if whoever was supposed to be looking after them had neglected to let them out . . . which, in this case, was Dad.

Me and Mum both spotted the dog poo on the hallway carpet at the same time, and we both saw Jesus skulking guiltily into the kitchen, and we both knew whose fault it was.

'Oh, Dad . . .' I sighed.

'John!' Mum called out angrily.

There was no answer.

But we knew Dad was in, because we could hear voices coming from the front room – Dad's voice, and some others that I didn't recognize. When I looked at Mum, she closed her eyes in exasperation and slowly shook her head, and I knew we were both thinking the same thing – that Dad was in the front room getting drunk with a bunch of his drunk/ druggy friends, and because he was drunk he'd forgotten all about Jesus and Mary.

Of course, it didn't really matter that Jesus had pooed on the floor. I mean, it wasn't like a disaster or anything. But letting it happen, and making Jesus feel guilty about it when it wasn't his fault . . . well, it was just such a lousy thing for Dad to do – so thoughtless and selfish and stupid. And what was even more idiotic about it was that Dad was already in Mum's bad books anyway. Which is why I wasn't at all surprised when Mum shoved open the door and went marching into the front room, her fists clenched, her eyes narrowed, her anger about to explode . . .

But the explosion never happened.

Instead, as I followed Mum into the room, I saw her stop suddenly and say 'Oh,' in a taken-aback kind of way, as if she'd just seen something she hadn't expected to see, and when I moved to her side and looked into the room, I knew exactly how she felt.

Dad *was* drunk, and he *wasn't* alone, but the people in the room with him were nothing like the drunk/druggy people we'd both imagined. There were three of them – two men and a woman. The men were sitting on the settee, the woman was in the armchair, and Dad was sitting cross-legged on the floor in front of them. The men (both in their twenties) were pale-faced and wore cheap black suits, and the woman (who was about sixty) was dressed in a brown woollen jacket and a long black smocky kind of skirt. They all had Bibles in their hands, and they all had those simpering God-seller smiles on their faces.

Dad was smiling too.

And he had a Bible in his hand.

And his eyes . . .

God, his eyes.

Although they were the same old booze-addled eyes that I'd got to know so well – unfocused, reddened, puffy, dull – they somehow weren't *his* eyes any more. They were the eyes of someone who thinks they've found the answer to everything.

It was terrifying.

About a week after that, Dad sobered up.

Stopped drinking.

Stopped taking drugs.

And replaced them both with God.

(i'm going to the darklands)

That was the worst time for me, when Dad became a God addict. For the first few weeks, all he ever did – day and night – was sit in the front room reading the Bible. He stopped eating, stopped going out, stopped washing, stopped changing his clothes. And the only time he ever slept was when he physically couldn't keep his eyes open any longer. All he did, hour upon hour, was sit there like a man possessed (which I guess he was), devouring every single word of the Bible. Occasionally he'd mutter and mumble to himself as he underlined particular passages or scribbled tiny notes in the margins, but most of the time he was silent.

And that wasn't my dad.

That was someone else.

Some*thing* else.

Another dad.

Even when he started getting back to some of his old ways – going out again, mixing with the wrong people again . . . boozing again – he still wasn't my dad any more. He'd start drinking (and reading the Bible) as soon as he woke up now, glugging down the remains of last night's bottle, and he wouldn't stop drinking (and reading the Bible) until he passed out. It was almost as if he'd become some kind of born-again alcoholic. Like he'd found whatever he was looking for – he'd found his salvation – through drinking again, only now it was all mixed up with God, like some kind of abominable cocktail. And it was the God part of the cocktail that really ripped me apart. I mean, I'd never *liked* it when he'd been just a junky or just an alcoholic, but at least then he'd still been my dad. Even when he was totally whacked out of his head, he'd still have *some* of his Dadness left. But now he'd found God . . . well, it just seemed to suck all the Dadness out of him. It sucked everything out of him – his mind, his soul, his life, his love . . .

I hated it.

Mum hated it.

'It's killing him,' she told me once.

And she was right.

But that wasn't the end of it . . .

*(oh something won't let me
go to the place
where the darklands are)*

Reason Four: There is no <u>Reason Four</u>.

head (1)

I'm still sitting on my bed with Jesus and Mary, still lost in my head with my Dad-thoughts and my God-thoughts and the drowning beauty of The Jesus and Mary Chain swirling darkly around the room, when all at once the dogs' ears prick up and they both jump off the bed and start yapping away like crazy at the bedroom door. It's their someone-at-the-front-door bark (*ROWROWROWROWROWROWROW*), which is kind of surprising because the clock on my bedside table says 22:39 . . . not that that's *late* or anything. I mean, when Dad was here we'd get people calling round at all times of the night. But Dad isn't here any more. And me and Mum don't get too many visitors, especially at this time of night.

Hence the surprise.

Anyway, by the time I've got off the bed and turned the music down and let Jesus and Mary out, and they've gone careering down the stairs (*ROWROWROWROWROWROWROW*), I can already hear Mum opening the front door and cautiously saying hello to someone.

'Who is it, Mum?' I call out, starting down the stairs.

I can't really hear much over the excited barking, but what I can hear doesn't sound too bad. I mean, it doesn't *sound* like someone Mum doesn't want to see (she's been dreading a visit from the police ever since Dad disappeared).

'Mum?' I call out again, nearing the bottom of the stairs. 'Are you all right? Who is it?'

Whoever it is, she's letting them in now. And Jesus and Mary aren't barking any more, they're just kind of squiggling around in the doorway, wagging their tails, whining and groaning in doggy delight.

'It's some friends of yours,' Mum says, stepping unsteadily to one side and smiling dopily at me. (*Friends of mine?* I think to myself.) She turns back to whoever's at the door and ushers them inside. 'Go on in,' she tells them.

And in they come – a bad-assed vision of flat bellies and breasts and clinking carrier bags – Mel Monroe and Taylor Harding.

'Hey, Dawn,' Taylor grins. 'How's it going?'

(*What?*)

'Yeah,' says Mel. 'Y'all right?'

I can't speak. I just stand there at the foot of the stairs, staring dumbly at them as they move along the hallway towards me. Taylor peers into the front room as she passes by, giving it a quick once over, and Mel's eyes are kind of flicking around too, taking everything in. Behind them, I can see Mum closing the front door and giving me a vague nod of approval, as if to say – *well done, Dawn, it's good to see you've got some friends at last*. And I want to tell her – *no, these aren't my friends . . . I don't even want them to be here*. But Taylor's standing right in front of me now, and all I can do is look up into her eyes and see the hardness beneath the smile.

'So,' she says quietly. 'D'you fancy a drink then?'

(walk away
you empty head)

Taylor starts jabbering at me as I reluctantly lead them upstairs to my room. 'The party got blown out,' she tells me. 'Mel's mum came back, so we had to call it off. We just thought we'd better come round and let you know, you know? We would've rung you, but we don't know your number . . .'

I'm not really listening to her (although I'm listening enough to wonder why she's gone back to the story about the party being at Mel's place rather than hers), I'm just kind of filled with a belly-wobbling mixture of strangeness, confusion, and unwanted curiosity. I don't *want* to be curious about what they're doing here. I don't want to be *anything* about it. I just want them to be gone. *Please*, I want to say, *get out of my house, leave me alone. I don't want you to be here.*

But I don't have the guts to say anything.

Instead, as Taylor is still yapping away – '. . . and as we were coming round here anyway, we thought we might as well bring something to drink . . . you know, like it's a shame to waste it . . .' – I open my bedroom door and they follow me inside.

Jesus and Mary scuttle in behind them and jump up on the bed.

'Head' is still playing quietly on my PC.

'Nice,' says Taylor, looking around at all my stuff.

'Yeah,' Mel agrees.

I don't know if they mean it or not, but I wouldn't be surprised. I've got some pretty nice stuff. I've got (among

55

other things) an Arbico 880 GTX PC with a 20.1-inch flat-panel screen, a Sony Vaio Blu-ray laptop, a nice little 19-inch flatscreen TV, a 30GB iPod touch, a Samsung i320 mobile ... I've got all kinds of good things. (That's all they are though – things. And in twenty years' time they won't even be that. They'll just be a pile of old shit.)

But, anyway, as Taylor and Mel are looking around at my stuff, I'm kind of secretly looking at them, and I've almost stopped wondering what they're doing here now. They're here, and that's that. And that's enough for me to deal with for the moment. So I'm just kind of looking at them, you know? Their faces, their eyes, their clothes ...

I'm not all that good with clothes (clothes are just clothes to me, just something to cover up my lumpiness), but, as far as I can tell, Taylor and Mel are both wearing the same clothes they had on this afternoon. Short things, tight things, things that show off their delectable bodies. And as I'm looking at them, I'm reminded, embarrassingly, of the pictures of Eve in my *Children's Illustrated Bible* (although I doubt very much if Taylor and Mel have ever used apples as a means of temptation).

The thought of Eve suddenly reminds me of something else, and as Taylor sits herself down on the edge of the bed and Mel goes over to join her, I casually stroll over and (equally) casually pick up the Bibles from the bed, at the same time giving the duvet a quick pat down, as if I'm not doing anything at all, you know ... I'm not trying to *hide* anything. I'm not *embarrassed* about anything. What have I got to be embarrassed about? Me? Embarrassed? No, I'm just ... you know, I'm just tidying up.

'Is that what you bought this afternoon?' asks Mel, eyeing the Bibles in my hand.

'Uh, yeah . . .' I shrug. 'It's nothing . . . just a project for school.'

'What kind of project?'

'Religious Studies,' I tell her, putting the Bibles away in the drawer of my bedside cabinet.

'Fucking religion,' says Taylor. 'Waste of fucking time.' She takes a packet of cigarettes from her pocket and looks over at me. 'All right if I smoke?'

'You can set yourself on fire if you want,' I tell her.

It's a dumb thing to say – not even funny really – and Taylor doesn't react, she just lights her cigarette and reaches into the carrier bag at her feet and pulls out a half-bottle of vodka. She unscrews the cap, takes a gulp, then offers the bottle to me.

'Want some?'

'No, thanks.'

'Why not?'

I just shrug.

She picks up the carrier bag. 'I've got a bottle of WKD Blue if you prefer –'

'No, it's all right,' I say. 'I'm fine, thanks.'

'Don't be stupid,' she says, waving the bottle of vodka at me. 'Go on, have a drink . . . it's not going to kill you.'

I shake my head. 'No, really . . .'

She frowns at me. 'What the fuck's the matter –?'

'She said she doesn't want any,' Mel interrupts, snatching the bottle from Taylor's hand. 'If she doesn't want any, she doesn't want any. All right?' She stares at Taylor for a moment, then – after a quick grin at me – she takes a hefty slug from the bottle.

Taylor shakes her head, bemused, as if she's never met anyone who's refused a drink before. She takes a puff on her cigarette and breathes out smoke. Jesus, sitting beside her, sniffs, blinks his eyes, lifts his head, and sneezes. Mary gives him a startled look. Mel laughs. Taylor clamps the cigarette between her lips and playfully gives Jesus a two-handed rub on his snout.

Jesus wags his tail.

I go over to my computer desk, empty out a mug full of pens, and pass the empty mug to Taylor to use as an ashtray.

She smiles tightly at me. 'I bet your mum wouldn't say no to a drink.'

I go over to the window and open it up a bit to let the cigarette smoke out.

'She likes a bit of grass too, doesn't she?' Taylor continues. 'I could smell it on her clothes.'

'So?' I shrug again.

She shrugs back at me. 'Nothing . . . I was just saying, that's all.'

'What?'

'Nothing.' She grins at me for a moment, then flicks her cigarette ash into the mug and turns her attention to Jesus and Mary.

'What's their names?' she says.

'Sorry?'

'The dogs – what are they called?'

I give her the story about naming the dogs after The Jesus

and Mary Chain, how they're my favourite band, blah blah blah, and both Taylor and Mel seem to find it genuinely amusing that my dogs are called Jesus and Mary. And the weird thing is, as they're giggling and snorting about it, I actually find myself enjoying their laughter. It makes me feel good. It gives me confidence. It's like they're impressed with me, and for some pathetic reason that gives me a boost.

'So,' says Mel, cadging a cigarette off Taylor. 'Is that what's playing now – this music, I mean. Is this The Jesus and Mary whatsit?'

'Chain,' I tell her. 'Jesus and Mary *Chain*. Yeah . . .' I go over to my desk and tweak up the volume on the PC speakers. The sound of 'Head' screeches and howls from the speakers.

> (*i think you're crawling up my spine*
> *i think you're crawling up my spine*
> *hey hey hey*
> *hey hey hey*
> *don't want you to stay*
> *want you to stay*)

'What do you think?' I ask Taylor and Mel. 'Do you like it?'

Mel shrugs. 'It's all right, I suppose. Are they new?'

'New?'

'Yeah, are they a *new* band?'

'No . . . I think they first started in the eighties –'

'Christ,' spits Taylor, pulling a face. 'Haven't you got anything else?'

'No,' I mutter (and I can feel my good feeling, my boosted confidence, beginning to deflate).

'What about some Lily Allen?' Taylor says. 'Or Kanye West or Mika or something? I mean, shit . . .' She shakes her head, waving her hand dismissively at the speakers. 'This is fucking *awful.*'

'Yeah, well,' I mumble. 'If you don't like it –'

'Nice system though,' she says, ignoring me. 'The PC, I mean.' She drops her cigarette into the mug, takes another glug of vodka, and passes the bottle to Mel. 'Must have cost you a bit,' she says to me.

'What?'

'The PC . . . all this stuff.' She waves her hand again. 'And that TV you've got downstairs . . . I mean, you must be doing all right.' She grins at me. 'Unless it's all nicked, of course.'

I don't say anything to that, I just look over at Mel (for no reason at all, as far as I know – I just find myself looking over at her). She's sitting with her legs crossed, sipping demurely from the bottle of vodka, and there's something about her dark almond eyes – something about the way she's looking at me – that makes me feel kind of stupidly shy. She's wearing a low-cut cropped black vest that says *GLORIOUS* (in gold lettering) on the front, a pair of very short and very tight blue denim shorts, and Rocket Dog shoes emblazoned with the words *SEXY ARMY*. She's got bangles on her wrists, rings on most of her fingers, dangly plastic earrings, and a fine gold necklace round her neck. Her hair is kind of crimsony-black, shiny and curly, bunched up at the top but with a few long strands hanging loose. She's got beautiful olive skin, and her teeth are quite small and very very white.

60

'What?' she says, raising her eyebrows at me. 'What are you looking at?'

I shake my head and lower my eyes.

Taylor sniffs. 'So what does your old man do then?'

I look at her.

'Sorry?'

'Your dad . . . what does he do? Where's he get all the money to buy all this stuff for you?'

I glance at Mel. She's still just sitting there, smoking her cigarette, giving me that almond-eyed look. I turn back to Taylor. 'My dad's not here any more,' I tell her.

'What d'you mean?' she says. 'Your parents split up?'

'No . . . my dad just . . . he disappeared.'

'Disappeared?'

'Yeah . . .'

I really don't want to talk about this. It's my business, Mum's business . . . it's ours. It's nothing to do with anyone else. We don't even talk about it ourselves.

It's too difficult.

Too close, too complicated.

'What do you mean, disappeared?' Taylor says, leaning forward, all wide-eyed and *interested*. 'He just left or something?'

'Yeah,' I sigh. 'Kind of . . . I mean, he just . . . he just went out one night and never came back.'

'When was this?'

'Couple of years ago.'

'And you've never heard from him since?'

'No.'

'No shit,' she says, glancing at Mel. 'What a fucker, eh?'

61

Mel nods, still looking at me. 'What do you think happened to him, Dawn? Do you think he just did a runner or something? I mean, was he, you know ... like, was he seeing someone else or something?'

I shrug. 'I don't know ...'

'What did your mum do? When he left, I mean ... did she look for him?'

'Of course she did. She didn't know where he'd gone ... she was worried to death. She looked everywhere, called everyone she knew ... she even called the police eventually.'

'Why?' says Taylor.

I glare at her. 'Why do you think? No one knew where he was. He could have had an accident or something, or someone might have ...'

'Might have what?' Taylor says.

I shrug again. 'I don't know ... he might have got into trouble with someone.'

'What kind of trouble?'

I'm getting really pissed off with this now. All these questions ... I mean, why the hell are they asking me all these questions about my dad? What are they trying to do to me?

(i think you're crawling up my spine)

I look at Mel

(want you to stay)

and then at Taylor

62

and Taylor says, 'Was he up to something?'

'Up to something?'

'Yeah,' she grins, tapping the side of her nose. 'You know ... *up* to something.'

'Like what?'

'You tell me.'

I stare at her, suddenly sick to death of everything about her: her long face, her blondie-blonde hair, her stupid red lips, her flashy-lashed too-blue eyes. Her voice, too, is really getting on my nerves. She talks like a seabird with a really bad cough – *ack ack yackack ack.*

'What's the matter?' she says to me now (*wacksamacka?*). 'You got a problem or something?' (*yackacka wacka asamack?*)

'Yeah,' I say, still staring at her. 'I've got a problem.'

'Yeah?'

I'm probably about to say 'Yeah,' again, but before I get the chance, Mel gives Taylor a sharp little dig with her elbow and says, 'Leave it out, Tay.'

'I'm only –' Taylor starts to explain.

'Yeah, I know,' Mel says, cutting her off. 'You got a cigarette?'

Taylor looks annoyed for a moment, but then she just shrugs and lobs her packet of cigarettes to Mel. Mel catches the packet, takes one out and lights it.

'I need a piss,' Taylor says to me, getting to her feet. 'Where's the toilet?'

'Downstairs, end of the hallway, on your right.'

She goes out, adjusting her bra strap with her thumb as she goes, and a few seconds later Jesus and Mary hop off the bed and follow her down the stairs. I wonder for a moment if I ought to call out after her – 'Don't worry about the dogs, Taylor, they're not following you, they just need to go out for a wee. You don't have to do anything, they'll let themselves out through the dog flap in the back door.' But by the time I've thought about it, Taylor's already downstairs, and she probably doesn't give a shit about the dogs anyway...

So now I'm on my own with Mel

(i think you're crawling up my spine)

and for a moment or two there's a strangely awkward silence between us. It's the kind of silence you get when you're left alone with someone who makes you feel stupidly shy. We both just sit there (me at my desk, Mel on the bed) not really knowing what to do (although it's probably just me that doesn't know what to do). And the silence gets bigger and bigger...

Until, eventually, Mel takes a puff on her cigarette and says, 'Don't worry about Taylor. She doesn't mean anything. She's just being...'

'Being what?'

Mel smiles. 'She's just being Taylor.'

I'm not really sure what that means, but I smile and nod as if I do.

Mel leans back and rubs the back of her neck. 'So,' she says, 'this project you're doing, the thing with the Bibles... what's it about?'

Project? I think for a moment. *What project?* And then I realize what she means, and I quickly have to think of an answer. 'Oh, right, the project. Yeah . . . well, it's nothing really, just something about God, you know . . . the Old Testament and all that. I haven't really started it yet.'

Mel nods. 'What do you think about it? I mean, all that religious stuff . . . God and Jesus, priests and vicars and everything?'

I look at her, suddenly realizing that I'm sitting in my bedroom talking to Mel Monroe about God.

Q. How unlikely is that?
A. Very.

'My brother . . .' Mel says very quietly.
'What?'
She shakes her head. 'Nothing.'
'I didn't think you had a brother.'
'I don't.'

I look at her, not sure what's going on. She doesn't say anything for a while, she just sits there, staring blindly at the floor, as if she's totally alone . . . and then, all of a sudden, she kind of shivers, a momentary little shake of her body, and that seems to snap her out of it (whatever *it* is). She takes a long drag on her cigarette and lets the smoke out with a sigh.

'Yeah, anyway,' she says, her voice suddenly quite cold. 'Do you want to turn that music off now? It's really starting to get on my tits.'

I shrug – 'OK' – and click on the *stop* button.

The room goes quiet.

No music, no soundtrack.

I can hear the faint sound of the TV downstairs.

Voices.

A door opening, closing.

I glance at the clock. 23:42.

Taylor and Mel have been here for over an hour.

'Is your mum all right?' Mel asks me.

'Yeah . . . why shouldn't she be all right?'

Mel shrugs. 'I was only asking.'

'Yeah, well . . .'

And that seems to be the end of our conversation for now.
Mel just sits there with her legs crossed, smoking her cigarette, jiggling a foot up and down. And I just sit there in the
unfamiliar silence, asking myself questions.

Why is Taylor taking so long?

What did Mel mean about her brother?

And how come she keeps flipping from Almost Quite
Nice to Definitely *Not* Nice?

And what did Taylor mean about my dad? (*What a fucker,
eh? Was he up to something?*)

(My name is Dawn.

I'm thirteen years old.

My name is Dawn.

I don't want to think about it.)

'You all right?'

I open my eyes and look at Mel. 'What?'

'You went a bit funny there for a minute . . .'

'Funny?'

'I thought you'd fallen asleep.'

'What's so funny about that?'

She frowns at me. 'Nothing. I just meant...'

She stops talking as Taylor comes flouncing back into the room.

'All right?' she says.

Mel nods at her.

Jesus and Mary waddle in and jump on the bed.

Taylor grins at me. 'Does your mum always watch late-night horror films? I mean, she's sitting down there watching *Creepshow 2*, for Christ's sake.'

'So?' I say.

Taylor shrugs and looks over at Mel. 'You ready?'

Mel nods again and starts getting to her feet.

Taylor turns back to me. 'We'll see you later then, all right?'

'Yeah,' I say (although I'm not really sure what she means. Does she *really* mean they'll see me later? Or is she simply saying goodbye?)

As Mel gives the dogs a farewell scratch on the head, I get up from the desk and move over to the door. Taylor picks up the bottle of vodka and puts it back in the carrier bag – *clink* – and Mel looks around the room for a second or two, checking that she hasn't left anything behind. And then they both just waltz on out the door.

I follow them.

Down the stairs.

Along the hallway.

The door to the front room is closed, but Taylor still calls out, 'See you later, Mrs B,' as we go past it. Then we get to the front door, and I'm thinking I'd better be nice and polite and open the door for them, but Taylor's already turning the handle and opening it (as if she's opened it a million times before).

A mist of cold rain hazes across the doorway, silver and orange in the street-lit darkness, and from somewhere down the street I can hear the sound of a car starting up and driving away.

'See you then,' says Taylor, stepping out into the night.

Mel says nothing, just gives me a strange little smile.

And then they're both gone, clacking away down the rain-blown pavement, huddled up close to each other, their voices stealing away into the night.

(walk away
you empty head)

Mum's pretty zonked out when I go into the front room. Her eyes are half closed, her head slumped down on her chest, and the cigarette in her hand has burned down to the filter. As I take the tube of ash from her hand and drop it into an ashtray, she lifts her head, trying to focus her eyes, and she smiles unsteadily at me.

'All right?' I ask her, sitting down on the arm of the chair.

She nods.

I glance at the TV. *Creepshow 2* must have finished, or maybe Mum just got fed up with it, because now she's watching one of those police–camera–car-chase programmes. The sound's on mute. There's a car chase going on – night-vision, filmed from a helicopter, two white blobs speeding along through a blur of grey.

'Did Taylor talk to you when she was down here?' I ask Mum.

'Hmm . . .?' she murmurs, staring at the TV screen.

'Taylor . . . the blonde girl. Did she come in here and talk to you?'

'Taylor?'

'Yeah. The blonde girl.'

Mum nods (then almost immediately shakes) her head. 'Yeah, no . . . no, she didn't say very much. Just hello, you know . . . she seems all right. Said she liked the TV.'

'The TV?'

'Yeah, nice TV . . . that's what she said. Nice TV.'

'Right . . .' I pause for a moment or two, gazing absently at another car chase on the TV screen (this one filmed from inside the chasing police car), then I turn back to Mum and say, 'She didn't ask you anything about Dad, did she?'

Mum goes still. 'What about him?'

'Nothing . . . it's just that Taylor was being really nosy, that's all. Asking all sorts of questions about Dad and stuff. I just wanted to make sure that she hadn't been bothering you.'

With some difficulty, Mum sits up straight and looks at me. 'What kind of questions?'

I shrug. 'Just questions, you know . . . like what he does, that kind of thing.'

'What he *does*?'

'It's nothing to worry about, Mum . . . it's just the kind of

69

stuff people ask you about. You know – my dad works for so-and-so, what does *your* dad do?'

Mum frowns. 'Who's so-and-so?'

'Nobody. It's just . . . I'm just trying to explain what I mean.' I put my hand on her shoulder and smile at her. 'It's all right, Mum. Honestly . . . it doesn't matter. Just forget about it.'

She blinks at me, struggling to keep me in focus, and she tries to smile, but she's too drunk, too lost, too mixed up and sad. I lean down and kiss the top of her head. Her hair smells of cherries and smoke.

'Come on,' I tell her. 'Let's get you to bed.'

inside me (3)

Two years is a long time. Two years is no time at all. It's time enough for the cave in your head to grow so small that your breath feels like stone in your throat, but it's nowhere near time enough for you to forget who you are.

(i've seen my time away)

The last time I saw my dad was on a snowy December morning just over two years ago.

(it's living inside me)

I'm in the front room wrapping up a Christmas present for Mum, and Jesus and Mary are sitting on the floor beside me, their eyes fixed intently on the box in my hand. Inside the box is one of those Cow-In-A-Can things. You know, it's like a little round tin with a perforated top, and when you turn it upside down it makes a mooing noise. Which Jesus and Mary find fascinating, and fascinating to them means worth chewing up, so I'm trying to wrap the Cow-In-A-Can without turning it upside down, so they don't hear the mooing.

Mum's out shopping somewhere.

And I can hear Dad coming down the stairs – *cough cough, shuffle shuffle, cough cough* – and now I can feel myself coming apart. There's two of me now. Me and me. Two selves. And while *my* heart beats faster and *my* throat tightens and *my* hands start shaking with fear, I can feel the other me cowering away in the safety of her cave.

My name is Dawn.

My belly hurts.

My name is Dawn.

I can't move.

All I can do is sit here listening to the sound of Dad's hungover footsteps coming down the stairs . . . the sound of his unsteady feet, his trembling hand holding on to the banister, his bloodshot eyes, his unshaven face, his soured breath, his hopelessness . . .

His terrible shame.

He won't talk to me any more.

He won't come in here and smile at me and ask me what I'm doing. His eyes won't light up when I show him the Cow-In-A-Can. He won't pick up Jesus in one hand and Mary in the other and lift them up to his face and blow raspberries at them. He won't even call out goodbye to me.

He won't do anything.

Not any more.

'Dad!' I call out, trying to get to my feet. 'Dad!'

But my legs are dead from sitting on the floor for too long, and it takes me a while to get up without falling over, and by the time I've crossed the room and opened the door and gone out into the hallway, Dad's already halfway out the front door.

'Dad!' I yell again.

And just for a moment, he pauses.

Half a moment.

And in that fraction of a moment I see (for ever) a hunched and unwashed figure in a ragged old duffel coat. I see a gaunt head hidden in the folds of a hood, a glimpse of yellowed skin, a dark flash of desperate eyes, and then, without a word, he's gone.

Dad didn't come home that night, and he didn't come home the next night either. Mum wasn't too concerned. This wasn't the first time he'd gone missing for a couple of days, and he'd always come back before. He'd be out getting drunk somewhere, that was all. Getting drunk, sleeping it off, getting drunk again, sleeping it off . . .

He'd be back when he ran out of money.

But two days soon became three days.

And three days turned into four.

And that's when Mum started worrying.

She called all his friends (or his 'so-called friends', as she insists on calling them), but no one seemed to have seen him for a while. And because most of the people he knew were as messed up and constantly wrecked as he was, most of them couldn't remember when or where they'd last seen him either. And even if they could remember, they were so junkily paranoid about telling the truth it was barely worth asking them *anything*. I mean, if you ask people like that what day it is, they'll lie to you. And then there were the other people

73

that Dad sometimes hung around with – the *real* bad guys: drug dealers, suppliers, thieves, gangsters, villains. The kind of people who won't tell you anything about anything.

Mum tried them all, but without any luck.

No one had seen Dad. No one knew where he was. No one knew anything.

Mum tried the hospital . . . nothing.

She went looking for him – traipsing around town, going to all the clubs and the pubs and the bars, showing people his photograph, talking to bar staff and bouncers and anyone else who'd listen . . .

Nothing.

A lot of them *knew* Dad – they knew who he was, they remembered seeing him around . . . but not recently. Not in the last week or so.

Dad, it seemed, had simply vanished.

And so eventually – and against all her instincts – Mum went to the police station and reported him missing. I went with her, of course, and I was surprised to find that the police actually took us quite seriously. They recorded all Dad's details on a special form, including a full physical description, any special circumstances leading up to his disappearance (none, according to Mum), and his current mental state (alcoholic). They also asked us for a recent photograph, which Mum had forgotten to bring. But they said not to worry, they'd get someone to pick it up later when they came round to search our house.

'Search our house?' Mum said, surprised. 'Why do you want to search our house?'

'It's just routine, Mrs Bundy,' the police officer explained.

'You'd be surprised how many so-called missing persons turn up safe and sound in their own homes.'

'But he's *not* at home,' Mum said. 'I know he's not —'

'I understand, Mrs Bundy,' the officer said. 'But, as I said, it's just routine.'

'Right . . .' Mum said hesitantly. 'So when will you be doing that then?'

'The sooner the better. How does first thing tomorrow morning sound?'

I've learned quite a lot since then. For example, I know that if you report a person missing, and that person is an adult, and if the police eventually find him (or her), but he (or she) doesn't want their whereabouts known, the police have to respect those wishes – i.e. if you run away from home as a grown-up, no one can make you go back. I've also learned that although the police take every missing person report very seriously, there are some they take more seriously than others. Kids, of course, especially really young kids. Vulnerable people (whatever that means). Old people. Which is all fair enough. But it kind of means that if your dad goes missing, and he's not much to shout about – he's a drunk, an ex-junkie, he's got a prison record – well, the police aren't going to spend all that much time looking for him. I mean, they're not going to put Sherlock Holmes on the case, are they?

No.

They're not really going to do very much at all.

Another thing I've learned is that Mum knew a lot more about Dad's dodgy dealings than I imagined. Which is why she was so worried when she found out that the police were going to search our house. Because, basically, there was all kinds of stuff hidden away in the house that she didn't want the police to find – drugs, pills, smuggled booze and cigarettes, stolen iPods, mobile phones, credit cards, trainers, T-shirts . . .

And it was while she was scouring the house for all this stuff, trying to get rid of it all before the cops came round . . . that's when she found the holdall. It was hidden away beneath Mum and Dad's bed. A dark-green holdall.

'What's that?' I asked Mum as she pulled it out.

She shook her head, looking puzzled. 'No idea. I've never seen it before.'

'Is it Dad's?'

'I don't know.'

She was kneeling on the floor beside the bed, and I was sitting on the bed looking down at her. She glanced at me for a moment, then turned back to the holdall and unzipped it.

'*Christ*,' she whispered.

'What is it?' I asked, leaning forward to peer into the bag.

Mum didn't answer, but she didn't have to. I could see what was inside the holdall now. It was money. Lots of it. Stacks and stacks of £20 notes and £50 notes. And nestling heavily on top of all the cash was a matt-black automatic pistol.

something's wrong (1)

We still don't know anything about the money. We still don't know where Dad got it from, or why he left it here. We still don't know if he left it here *for* us (which would mean that he knew he wasn't coming back), or if he just left it here for safe-keeping, to pick up sometime later...

We just don't know.

All we know is...

The money's ours now.

£183,480 in cash.

When we first found the holdall and counted the money, it totalled £222,560. But that was two years ago, and we've spent some since then. I mean, we haven't gone crazy with it or anything, but we've got ourselves what we want – TVs, PCs, laptops, etc. – and most of the time now we just use it to live on. If we didn't have it, we'd probably still get by. But getting by would mean living on Mum's (fraudulently claimed) Incapacity Benefit, and I think (rightly or wrongly) that we've both got enough to put up with without having to worry about counting pennies all the time.

And besides...

It's our money.

It might not make us feel any better about things, but it's a lot easier to feel bad about things with a big bunch of money under the floorboards than without.

Q. And the gun? Did you keep the gun?
A. Yes.
Q. Why?
A. No reason, really. It's just easier to keep it than get rid of it.

these days (1)

Every night, before I go to sleep, I write some words in a notebook. I don't know if these things I write are poems or not (and, to be honest, I don't really care). I just write them, whatever they are.

Tonight I write:

her chamber opens
and her eyes crawl out of her cave
and her eyes
crawl out through the tunnels
that connect her head to the rest of the world
and
when it's dark
you can see yourself

deep one perfect morning (1)

OK, it's ten o'clock Wednesday morning now (the morning after Taylor and Mel came round) and I'm out in the back garden with Jesus and Mary. It's a really nice day – kind of cold and windy, but bright-skied too – and the dogs are making the most of it. They're both scurrying around in excited circles, snorting as they go, sniffing up the stories in the wind. And I'm just standing here with my head full of music, and I'm watching the dogs, smiling at them, wondering what they can smell, and if they know what it is, and if they even care . . . and I decide to join in with their sniffing. So I lift my head up to the sky and breathe in deeply through my nose, snorting in a great lungful of air . . . but I sniff too hard, and a bit of snot gets sucked into my throat, and then I'm doubled over, hands against the wall, coughing and retching and spitting out lumps of snot and goo . . .

And there on the path at my feet, right where I'm spitting, are three empty snail shells.

Three raggedy shells, lined up in a raggedy line.

Each of them painted with a faded fluorescent letter.

Left to right, they read: *O, D, G.*

(There's a hole in the *D* shell (probably pecked out by a

thrush) and the bottom bit of the *D* is missing, so it's *possible* it could be a *B* . . . but I'm pretty sure it's not.)

'Uh?' I hear myself say.

I crouch down for a closer look. And, yes, they're definitely the snail shells I painted letters on last summer (I recognize the brushwork). And, yes, the *D* is definitely a *D*. And . . . uh? What are they doing here? How did they get here? Where have they been all this time? Why have they suddenly shown up today?

What the hell is going on?

ODG?

Is it a message?

Oh. Dee. Gee.

Who from?

Odigy.

I'm squatting down on the cracked concrete path now, with the cold wind chilling the back of my neck, and all I have inside my head are these three faded letters – *ODG* – and the six possible ways they can be combined: *ODG*, *DGO*, *GDO*, *DOG*, *OGD* and *GOD*.

The last one – *GOD* – is the scariest, of course. And I don't even want to think about that. I don't want to think that maybe God's sending me a message . . . that maybe he knows I'm trying to kill him, that maybe he's using his almighty powers to send me a Godly warning, a sign from above . . .

No, I don't want to think about that.

So I think about the other combinations of letters instead.

DGO, *GDO* and *OGD* (I think) don't mean anything to me at all.

ODG (I think) is the middle part of Spl*ODG*e, which *could* mean that he's been round here (when?) and spelled out his name with my painted snail shells (why and how?) and the *S*, *P*, *L* and *E* have somehow gone missing (how?) . . .

And *DOG* . . .?

I think about my dogs, wondering if the snail shells could be anything to do with them. I stand up, stiff-legged, and call out to them. 'Come here, dogs! Hey! Jebus . . . Mary! *HERE*!'

They ignore me.

I cup my hands to my mouth and shout out again, a lot louder this time. '*JEBUS! MARY! COME! HERE! NOW!*'

That does the trick. They stop their wind-crazed running around and they both come scampering up to me, looking a bit wary – heads down, tails wagging sheepishly – but as soon as I speak to them again – 'Good girl, good boy' – their heads lift up and they know that I'm not angry.

'What's this?' I say breezily to them, crouching down again and pointing out the snail shells. 'Come on, come and see . . .'

Jesus is braver than Mary, so he goes first – tiptoeing up to the snail shells, stretching out his neck, sniffing tentatively . . . and after a moment or two, when nothing has happened to him, Mary joins in with the sniffing. And I can tell by their cautiousness and their obvious lack of guilt that the snail shells are nothing to do with them. No, Jesus and Mary haven't dug out the shells (from some secret doggy hiding place) and laid them out on the path for me. They haven't tried to mess with my mind by misspelling the word DOG on the path.

And I feel a bit shameful (and stupid) for even considering it.

So, to make myself feel better, I reach out to give Mary a scratch on the head, but she's so intent on sniffing the shells that the sudden touch of my hand on her head makes her jump. And as she skitters off to one side, she steps on one of the shells, crunching it into the concrete, and her back foot flicks into the other two shells and sends them tumbling across the path. So now there's only two shells left intact, and instead of reading *ODG* they read *GO*.

So that's what I do.

I don't *really* think that Splodge has got anything to do with the snail shells, but there's a part of me that needs to find out (and I was going out anyway, so it's not as if I have to make a special journey to go and see him or anything). As I head on down the street towards his house, with my iPod on and Jesus and Mary (both wearing their coats) at my feet, I see the blue van with *Farthings Furniture* written on the side pulling away from the pavement and motoring up towards Whipton Lane. The engine is coughing and spluttering, and plumes of black smoke are spewing out from the exhaust pipe. I watch it for a moment, remembering Splodge's curiosity about it yesterday, and for a paranoid second or two I find myself wondering if the van has got anything to do with anything else – i.e. the snail shells, the God stuff, the thing with Taylor and Mel . . .

Of course, I know in my heart that there's no connection between any of these things – that the blue van is just a blue van, that Taylor and Mel are just screwing me around, that the sudden appearance of the snail shells is just one of those totally random things . . . you know, one of those bizarrely random coincidences that seem so unbelievably improbable that it's incredibly easy to assume that they're *not* random, that they *must* mean something, that something (or someone) *must* be responsible for them. But, as someone once said (I can't remember who it was) – *Yes, strange things happen. But it's a big world out there, there's a lot of stuff going on – it'd be strange if strange things* didn't *happen now and again*.

And, anyway, I know that God's *not* putting the frighteners on me for trying to kill him. Because:

(i) he doesn't exist

(ii) and even if he *did* exist (which he doesn't), and even if he *was* trying to frighten me (which he isn't), why would he do it with snail shells? Why not use a bolt of lightning or a plague of bats or something? And why, if he *was* using snail shells to send me a message, why did he get the letters in the wrong order? I mean, he's God, isn't he? If he can create an entire universe in seven days, it shouldn't be too hard for him to get three crappy snail shells in the right order, should it?

'What do you think, Jeeb?' I ask Jesus.

He looks up at me, smiling his dog-smile.

And I take his happy silence for agreement.

When I get to Splodge's house, Splodge, as always, is sitting on his doorstep in his parka, watching the world go by. His birthmark is really purpley today.

'Hey,' I say to him, turning off my iPod.

'Hey, Dawn,' he replies. 'You all right?'

'Yeah.'

He turns and smiles at Jesus and Mary. 'Nice coats,' he says.

Jesus and Mary wag their tails in agreement.

Splodge looks back at me. 'Where're you going?'

I shrug. 'Nowhere, really. Just wandering around, you know . . .'

He nods.

I smile at him, trying to work out how to broach the subject of snails. It's a tricky one. I mean, how do you ask an eleven-year-old kid with a half-purple face if he's been secretly collecting your painted snails, saving them up for months, then putting them back in your garden? How do you do that without making him think you're mad? Or without making him think that you think *he's* mad?

You lie to him, that's how.

'You know that van?' I say to him.

'What van?'

'The blue one. You know, the one we saw yesterday. You said you see it around all the time but you've never seen anyone get out of it.'

'Oh, yeah,' he says, nodding. 'The *Farthings Furniture* van. It went up the road a couple of minutes ago.' He looks at me. 'What about it?'

'I'm not sure,' I tell him, lowering my voice. 'But there was a van parked outside my house last night, and I think I saw someone sneaking into the alleyway that leads round to my garden.'

Splodge raises his eyebrows. 'Really?'

85

'Yeah.'

'What were they doing?'

'I don't know. I mean, it was dark. I couldn't really see very much. All I could make out was this shortish guy in a parka —'

'You saw him getting out of the van?'

'No . . . I just saw him going into the alleyway.'

'Did you call the police?'

I shake my head. 'He could have been anyone, a friend of one of my neighbours or something.'

Splodge frowns. 'You should have called the police.'

'Yeah, well,' I say. 'If I see him again, I will.'

I don't like lying to Splodge, but I don't dislike it enough not to do it. And, more to the point, it serves a purpose. Because now I *know* that Splodge didn't put the snail shells in my garden. Because, if he had, I would have seen the alarm in his eyes when I was telling him about the shortish guy in a parka who was skulking around my house last night. Because Splodge would have *been* that shortish guy in a parka.

But he wasn't.

I'm 99% sure of that.

So now all I'm left with, snail-shell-*and*-killing-wise, is GOD.

I put my earphones back in, hit the PLAY button, and head for the bus stop.

deep one perfect morning (2)

I get off the bus at the roundabout by the railway station and make my way through a rusted iron gate to a hedge-lined lane that runs parallel to the railway tracks. The lane is rutted with tractor tracks and murky brown puddles, but the ground in between the tracks is surprisingly firm, and I can walk it without too much trouble. Jesus and Mary run on ahead of me, sniffing around in the hedges, while I just take my time – walking steadily, listening to the music – as the lane leads me up into a quiet world of trees and fields and open skies.

It's OK.

I like it here.

It makes me feel *away* from things.

There are no bad-assy girls or mystery snails up here.

There's just:

- a big black rook swooping over a barren field towards a spindly line of winter trees on the bank of an invisible stream
- a train in the distance, rumbling silently out of the station
- occasional dried brown leaves, dislodged by the breeze, spiralling down from the wayside trees
- Dawn Bundy and her dogs.

I know this lane pretty well, I walk the dogs up here whenever I can, but I don't know anything about the church at the end of the lane. It's just a church, an old stone church with an old stone tower, surrounded by a tumbledown graveyard. And usually, when I get to the wooden gate that leads into the graveyard, I just turn round and start heading back. Not today though. Today I stop at the gate. And today, for the first time ever, I actually read the faded lettering on the wooden sign above the gate. It reads:

THE SECRET OF THE
LORD
IS WITH THOSE
WHO FEAR HIM,
AND HE WILL
SHOW THEM HIS
COVENANT

I look at it for a while, reading it through a couple of times, but it doesn't seem to make any sense, so I call the dogs and unlatch the gate and we go on into the graveyard. A curved path leads us along through the shadows of ancient trees and gravestones towards the front of the church, and as we follow the path I can smell the earthy scent of the dead leaves under my feet. I stop for a moment, looking down at the rotting leaves on the path, and I wonder . . .

Dead leaves.

Dead bodies.

These fallen leaves, I think to myself, they come from trees whose roots suck up stuff from the ground. And this is a graveyard. The ground here is full of dead people. Dead bodies, rotting flesh, leaking out God-knows-what into the soil – blood, dreams, brains, memories, emotions... and the roots of the trees are sucking up all this dead-body juice, and the juice is making the leaves, and the leaves themselves are crumbling and dying...

I could be standing on the remains of somebody's emotions.

I walk on.

There's a stillness to the air now, no sense of time. The old stone walls of the church look stern and sullen in the mid-morning light, and the flint-grey tower looms cold and dark against the bright January sky. The church door is set within a wooden-roofed entrance porch. It has a stone-tiled floor, a stone bench on either side, and stone walls hung with church and community notice boards. I stand there for a while, gazing idly at the messages:

CHRISTIAN STUDIES COURSE, WORSHIP FOR

THE YOUNG

BREAD AND CHEESE LUNCH

ARE YOU SUFFERING FROM ANXIETY AND

DEPRESSION? BEREAVEMENT?

DRUG AND ALCOHOL DEPENDENCY?

EMOTIONAL PROBLEMS?

CHURCH SERVICES FOR JANUARY AT

ST MICHAEL'S CHURCH:

MORNING SERVICE BEGINS AT 10.45

With Revd David Welchman and the

Soloist Martha Angstrom.

EVENING SERVICE STARTS AGAIN AT 6 P.M.

With Revd David Welchman and the Soloist Alan Taylor.

EVERYONE WELCOME

It doesn't actually say what *day* the church services are on, but I'm guessing it's probably going to be Sunday, and I suppose I should have realized that there won't be anything happening here today. I mean, it's not as if God needs worshipping *every* day of the week, is it?

But I'm here now, so I might as well try the door, just in case.

I try the door.

It's locked.

I stare uselessly at it – a big slab of heavy dark wood, giant-sized hinges, cast-iron bolts – and I try to imagine what's behind it. Silent church things, I suppose. Pews and pulpits. Stained glass. Darkness.

The unwelcoming smell of God.

At my feet, Mary lets out a troubled whine.

I look down at her. 'What's the matter? Don't you like it?'

She nervously wags her tail.

I smile at her. 'Too spooky for you?'

She yawns, embarrassed.

Beside her, Jesus barks quietly – letting me know that *he's* not afraid. He's fine. But if Mary wants to leave, well . . . that's fine with him too.

'Come on then,' I tell them. 'Let's go.'

We leave the porchway and follow the pathway back through the graveyard towards the gate. About halfway along the path, set back in a little flower garden, there's a wooden bench. It looks like a nice place to rest for a while, and my legs are kind of tired from all that walking, and it's not as if I'm in any great hurry to be anywhere else . . .

So I sit down.

And I gaze out over the graveyard, looking without thinking at the tombs and the crosses and the trees and the headstones . . .

And then I close my eyes and bow my head in thought.

psycho candy

I like being in this big black nowhere place. I could stay here
for ever, alone in my unworld, with my eyes closed and the
dark music playing, not being thirteen years old, not having
to *not* think about anything, just listening to this beautiful
nothingness . . .

But there's always something, isn't there? There's always
*some*thing that brings you back from your nowhere. And this
time it's a sudden touch – the touch of a finger tapping softly
on my shoulder – that jolts my heart and jerks me out of my
void. I gasp quietly, a startled breath, and my eyes spring
open, bombarding me with the too-bright dazzle of the
outside world, and there on the path in front of me is a
kindly-looking man in a beige corduroy jacket.

'I'm so sorry,' he says, as I fumble the earphones from my
ears. 'I didn't mean to frighten you.' He smiles, showing me
that he means no harm. 'Are you all right?'

He's not young, this man, but he's not old either. He's
probably somewhere between thirty and forty. Medium
height, medium size, medium just about everything. He has
a harmless-looking face, very ordinary light-brown hair and
totally average dull-brown eyes (that match the colour of the

battered old briefcase in his hand). Beneath his beige jacket, he's wearing a dull-black shirt with a white dog collar – you know, a vicar's collar. So, unless he's going to a fancy-dress ball, I'm guessing that he actually *is* a vicar. Or a priest, or a rector, or a curate or something. I don't really know the difference.

'What?' I say to him.

He smiles. 'I just wanted to make sure you were all right, that's all. I saw you sitting there, you see, and I thought perhaps you were ill or something...'

'No,' I tell him, looking around to see where Jesus and Mary are. 'No, I'm fine. I was just, you know ... I was just thinking.'

He nods, as if he understands. 'It's a good day for thinking.'

I spot Jesus and Mary sniffing around a headstone on the other side of the path, and I almost call out their names, but I stop myself just in time. I mean, this guy's a vicar, so he'd probably be offended if he knew my dogs were called Jesus and Mary. And although I don't care (because, as far as I'm concerned, it *isn't* offensive), there's no point in needlessly upsetting him, is there?

'Are they your dogs?' the vicar says to me.

'Yeah.'

I whistle them – once, twice – and they both come trotting over.

'They're beautiful,' the vicar says.

'Thanks.'

He watches them as they come up and sit down beside me, and I watch them too – wondering why they're just sitting

93

there quietly, with a hint of childish embarrassment in their eyes. Why aren't they doing what they usually do when they meet someone new? Why aren't they running round in circles, wagging their tails and whining their beautifully stupid little heads off?

'I'm David Welchman, by the way,' the vicar says. 'I'm the parish vicar here at St Michael's.'

'Right,' I say, nodding my head.

He nods too, smiling at me, and I think he's probably waiting for me to tell him my name. But I don't think I want to. I don't know why not. I just don't.

'What are you listening to?' he asks me, glancing curiously at the earphones in my lap. 'Anything I'd know?'

'Probably not.'

He nods his head in a middle-aged-man-talking-to-a-teenage-girl-about-music kind of way. I wind up my earphones and stuff them in my pocket with my iPod. The vicar smiles at me again.

A cold wind is beginning to blow now, whipping up piles of dead leaves into tiny brown tornadoes, and above the church a bank of grey clouds is looming heavily across the sky.

'Looks like rain,' the vicar says, gazing upwards.

And even as he says it, I feel the touch of a single drop of rain on my hand. It feels icy and hot, very big and very small, like a miniature storm on the head of a giant pin.

'Well,' the vicar says to me, hefting the briefcase in his hand. 'I must get on . . .'

'Can I talk to you about something?' I ask him.

'Sorry?'

'I'd like to talk to you about something.'

'Well, of *course*,' he says, not very convincingly. 'What is it you'd like to talk to me about?'

'God.'

I'm pretty sure the vicar doesn't really want to talk to me, but I'm also pretty sure that he can't say no. Because:

(a) It's his job to talk to people about God.

And (b) it's pouring with rain now, and it wouldn't be very Christian of him to leave a young girl outside on her own in a storm.

But (c) he's obviously got some stuff to do, some business-y/briefcase-y kind of stuff, and he'd much rather be doing that than talking to me.

And more importantly (d) he's a man, a middle-aged man, and I'm a teenage girl, and there's no one else around just now, and he probably thinks it's not very appropriate for a middle-aged man to be on his own with a teenage girl (even if that teenage girl *is* kind of round and lumpyish and non-delectable).

So what's he going to do?

Well, he's going to compromise, that's what he's going to do. He's going to say to me, 'Come on, let's get out of this rain,' and he's going to hurry along the path towards the church, holding his briefcase over his head, and me and Jesus and Mary are going to follow him, and when we get to the shelter of the stone porch, that's as far as he's willing to go.

'Sit down, please,' he says, flapping rain from his jacket.

I look at the locked door, then back at him. 'Can't we go inside?'

'Well,' he says carefully. 'I think it's probably best if we talk out here.'

'Why's that?' I reply knowingly, looking him straight in the eye.

It's a terrible thing to say, totally unnecessary, and the part of me that *is* me (the Now Dawn) regrets it almost immediately. And even the other part of me (the Cave Dawn – who I know gets a tiny kick of irrational satisfaction from seeing the squirm of discomfort in the vicar's dull-brown eyes), even she knows that we're not being fair.

But it's too late now.

(I'm sorry.)

I've already said it.

(Sorry.)

And there's nothing I can do to take it back. All I can do is lower my eyes and sit myself down on the cold stone bench and pretend that nothing happened.

(*What happened?*

Nothing. Nothing happened.

There is no Reason Four.)

'So,' the vicar says to me after a while. 'How can I help you?'

His voice is still quite kindly, but there's an edge of caution to it now. It sounds like the voice of a gentle man talking to a potentially violent lunatic.

I raise my eyes and look at him.

(Sorry.)

And then, trying to appear as perfectly normal as possible, I say to him, 'Is it wrong to keep bad things a secret?'

He gives me a concerned and slightly puzzled look. 'I'm not quite sure what you mean.'

'If you know that something is wrong,' I explain. 'I mean, if you know that someone has done something wrong, something that they shouldn't have done, but you don't tell anyone about it . . . is that wrong?'

'Well,' the vicar says, his voice very serious now. 'It all depends on what this person has done.' He looks at me. 'Is this a hypothetical question? Or are we talking about something that's actually happened?'

'Yeah, it definitely happened.'

'I see. And do you *know* this person who's done something wrong?'

'Yes.'

He looks at me again, more concerned than puzzled now. 'Can you tell me what sort of thing this person has done?'

'Something pretty bad.'

'Have they broken the law?'

'Yes.'

'Have they hurt anyone?'

'Yes.'

'Badly?'

'Yes.'

'How badly?'

'As bad as it gets.'

The vicar slowly shakes his head. 'And you're telling me that you know this person? You know what they've done?'

'Yeah . . . I know them. And I know what they've done. And it's bad . . . you know, it's against the law. It's *wrong*.' I look at the vicar. 'Do you think I should tell someone about it?'

'I think you'd be making a terrible mistake if you didn't.'

'Right ... so you think I should do something?'

'Absolutely.'

'You don't think I should just sit back and let it happen?'

'Of *course* not.'

I look at him. 'So how come it's all right for God to let it happen?'

'I'm sorry?'

'It's a criminal offence, isn't it?'

The vicar looks puzzled. 'What is?'

'Failure to report a crime ... it's against the law. It's illegal.'

'I'm sure it is —'

'So how come God gets away with it? I mean, he witnesses all kinds of horrible stuff, doesn't he? But he never does anything about it. He never tries to stop it. He never reports anything. He never calls the police.' I look at the vicar. 'If anyone else did that, they'd be arrested.'

'Well,' says the vicar. 'I think you're being slightly ridiculous now —'

'I know,' I say. 'But I'm right though, aren't I?'

The vicar smiles at me.

I smile back, imagining God being arrested and charged with a zillion counts of failure to report a crime. I imagine him having his almighty fingerprints taken, being interviewed by the police. I imagine him conferring with his lawyer. I imagine him on trial, standing in the dock, swearing to himself to tell the truth, the whole truth, and nothing but the truth ... so help me Me. I imagine him being taken away in a police van, taken away to jail. I imagine him being locked up in a cell, with a horrible little bed and a horrible little sink and a horrible little lidless toilet . . .

And I don't know why I'm doing all this.

I don't know why I bothered coming up here at all.

Know thine enemy?

I *have* no enemy.

There is no God.

And this man, this vicar . . . he's just a man. He's just an ordinary man (wearing a slightly silly collar) who believes in something that doesn't exist. There's no point in asking him questions. There's no point in talking to him.

I don't want to *talk* about God.

I just want to kill him.

The rain isn't falling quite so heavily now. Jesus is cautiously poking his snout round the corner of the church porch, sniffing the fresh scents spirited up by the rain, and Mary is just sitting quietly on the cold stone floor, staring doggedly at the vicar's right shoe. The vicar, meanwhile, is looking at me in that silently thoughtful way that people who think they know more than you do. He has his faith, I suppose. And I guess he means well. But I *know* that if I was an evil person, and I wanted to do something bad to him, his faith wouldn't do anything to stop me.

'What does he actually do?' I say to him.

'I'm sorry?'

'God . . . I mean, what does he actually *do*?'

'Well,' the vicar says slowly (he's very fond of saying 'well'), 'it's not really a question of what God *does* –'

'It is for me.'

'Well, I'm sorry, but it's not that simple.' He looks at me then, and I can tell by the soundless whirring of the cogs in his brain that he's about to start *sermonizing* at me . . . and I really don't want that.

'I think I'd better go,' I tell him, getting to my feet.

He looks at me, slowly nodding his head. 'Well . . . if you ever want to talk to me again about anything, anything at all . . .' He pauses, showing me the genuine concern in his eyes. 'I can't promise you any answers, but sometimes it just helps to talk.'

'OK.'

'No matter what you do or don't believe in.'

'Yeah . . . well, thanks. I'll bear that in mind.'

He smiles. 'Good.'

'I'll see you later,' I tell him.

'I hope so.'

And, with that, I'm gone.

shimmer

Q. How do you kill something that doesn't exist?
A. It depends.
Q. On what?
A. On who or what that non-existent thing is.

For example, if the non-existent thing you're trying to kill is:
   (1) Superman
then all you have to do is throw some kryptonite at him. But
if the non-existent thing you're trying to kill is:
   (2) a vampire
you could try all kinds of things, including:
   (a) driving an aspen, ash or whitethorn stake through its
heart with a single blow
   (b) firing a silver bullet blessed by a priest into its heart
   (c) pouring boiling water, boiling oil or holy water into
its grave
   (d) placing a coin in its mouth
   (e) decapitating it with an axe
   (f) burying it at a crossroads
   (g) chaining it to its grave with wild roses
   (h) boiling its head in vinegar

(i) cutting off its head and burning it

(j) driving a nail through its navel

(k) putting poppy seeds in its grave

(l) removing its heart and cutting it in two

(m) slicing off its toes and hammering a nail through its neck

or (n) putting a lemon in its mouth.

If, however, the non-existent thing you're trying to kill is:

(3) a werewolf (or any other kind of werebeast/ shapeshifter)

then you'd be better off:

(a) shooting it with a silver bullet

(b) cutting its heart out and burning it

(c) smashing its skull, then removing and destroying its head

(d) blowing it up (perhaps by tricking it into eating some explosive)

or (e) dropping it into a giant meat grinder.

OK, so if God was some kind of Superwerevampire and I wanted to kill him, then (in view of his *super*-supernatural resistance to death) I'd probably need to try all of the above, and that would mean getting hold of a whole load of stuff. I'd need:

- some kryptonite
- an aspen, ash or whitethorn stake
- a silver bullet
- a priest to bless the silver bullet
- a gun to fire the silver bullet (unless the silver bullet just happened to be the right kind of bullet for the pistol that Dad left behind, in which case (I presume) I could

use that
- some boiling water, boiling oil or holy water
- a coin
- an axe
- a shovel (or spade) for burying
- a crossroads (for burying at)
- a chain
- some wild roses
- vinegar
- two nails (both large enough for navel and neck)
- a hammer (for nailing)
- some poppy seeds
- a lemon
- some explosive
- a giant meat grinder.

Now (if you count the boiling water, the boiling oil and the holy water as three separate items, and the two nails as one), I make that twenty-one items in all. And out of those twenty-one items, I'd say that fourteen would be quite easy to get hold of, three would be quite difficult but possible, three would be virtually *im*possible, and one would definitely be impossible. Other impossibilities would include:
- locating God's grave
- locating his navel, neck, head, heart, mouth, toes, etc.
- locating anything about him full stop.

Q. How do you kill something that can't be located (because it doesn't exist)?
A. You look to where it *does* exist.

Q. Where does God exist?

A. In the pages of a book, and in the minds of billions of people.

Q. So where does that leave you?

A. God knows.

I can't kill billions of people, can I? I mean, even if I wanted to (which I don't), it simply isn't feasible.

No.

So, if killing billions of people isn't the answer, what *is* the answer? All I can think of right now (and right now, by the way, it's around six o'clock in the evening and I'm sitting on my bed with Jesus and Mary and we're surrounded by pages and pages of useless information taken from various sad websites, and it's raining outside and I've got 'Shimmer' playing incredibly loudly, over and over again) . . . and all I can think of right now is spending the rest of my life destroying every single Bible in the world . . .

And I really can't see that happening.

'Can you?' I ask Jesus and Mary.

Jesus is sleeping, so he doesn't answer. But Mary gives me a very small wag of her tail – just a one-off wigwag – and that tells me all I need to know.

'I'm wasting my time, aren't I?' I say to her.

yes

'I'm losing my way.'

yes

'I'm trying so hard to be all right that I'm making myself not be all right.'

yes

Q. What do you wish?
A. I wish I could reach inside my heart and make things never happen.

god help me (1)

My name is Dawn.

I'm thirteen years old.

My name is Dawn.

I don't want to think about it.

But every day it hurts more and more and the cave in my head gets smaller and smaller and the cave in my head gets darker and darker and the cave in my head gets colder and colder and if I don't get out of it soon, I think this cave is going to kill me.

Dawn is a daughter.

Dawn is a sex thing.

My name is Dawn.

I'm thirteen years old.

God help me.

her way of praying (2)

Downstairs, in the front room, Mum's in her armchair, smoking a cigarette and drinking her drink, and I'm on the settee, with Jesus and Mary snuggled up on either side of me, and we all seem to be watching *Zoo Vet at Large*. The curtained darkness of the room is illuminated with the flashing light of the monstrous TV, and every now and then, when the picture on the screen suddenly brightens, the TV light catches the cloud of cigarette smoke that's hanging beneath the ceiling, and just for a moment the cloud is a lightning cloud, and I'm not sitting in the front room any more, I'm sitting outside and a storm's about to break and I seem to be some kind of giant.

'Are you all right, love?' Mum says to me.

'Yeah,' I tell her. 'I'm fine.'

She picks up the TV remote and smiles at me. 'Do you want to watch something else?'

I shake my head. 'This is OK with me.'

'Sure?'

'Yeah.'

'I can see what else is on if you want.'

'No, really . . . this is fine.'

She looks at me for a moment, her head wobbling slightly, then she plucks her cigarette from the ashtray and turns her attention back to the TV. I watch her – sipping her drink, smoking her cigarette, staring glassy-eyed at the TV screen

(she's keeping time
keeping time)

and I wonder so much about her.

What are you thinking, Mum?
What's in your mind?
What are you feeling?
Do you feel anything at all any more?
Is there anything left of you?

I'm not sure if it's possible to love someone too much, but I think that's what happened with Mum. She loved Dad so much, so overwhelmingly, so totally without condition . . . she loved him so much, and she *still* loves him so much, that everything else means nothing.

Even her love for me.

That's not to say that her love for me isn't true, because it is. It's true, it's real, it's bigger than a planet. It's the only thing she cares about now. It's all she has left. But, even so, I still don't think it's big enough to change anything.

I could be wrong, of course.

I'm wrong about lots of things.

'You haven't forgotten I'm going to the doctor's tomorrow, have you?' Mum says to me now.

'No . . . your appointment's at five, isn't it?'

She nods.

I look at her. 'Do you want me to come with you?'

She smiles. 'No, I'll be all right, thanks.'

'Are you sure? I don't mind . . .'

She shakes her head. 'It's just a review . . .' (She mis-pronounces it, slurring her words – *juss-a-vuhvu* – but I know what she means (I speak fluent DrunkMumish). She has to see her doctor once every six months for a review of her prescriptions. The doctor doesn't do anything. He just asks her if everything's OK, she says yes, and that's about it.)

'I'll get the bus,' she says.

'Right.'

I look at her – cigarette, drink, remote control glued to her hand, dead eyes staring vacantly at TV adverts for stuff she couldn't care less about – and I wonder how long it's been since we actually talked to each other about anything. And, just like so many things, I can't remember. Or I don't want to remember. Or the Dawn that *can* remember doesn't come out of her cave any more.

'Are you OK, Mum?' I ask quietly.

'Hmm?' she says, her eyes still fixed on the TV screen.

'Are you OK?'

She looks at me, her face naturally blank for a moment, then she smiles and says, 'I'm fine.'

'Really?'

She nods, still smiling, but I think she knows that I'm not looking for a smile, and I think that scares her to death. Which is why I don't usually do anything about it. Because it's too hard for me to do anything else. Because that would be too hard for her.

It's what we do, every day of our lives: Mum smiles, I accept it, and everything's fine. We love each other. We don't have to talk. We don't have to go where the scary things are. It's what we do.

But today feels different.

I don't know why.

It just feels different.

'It's all right,' I tell her. 'I mean, I'm not trying to . . . you know . . . I'm only trying to . . .'

'I know,' she says. 'It's all right.'

'I just thought –'

'I'm fine.'

'Yeah, but you're not, are you? Not really.'

The way she stares at me for a moment, with a look of anaesthetized surprise on her face, it's as if she can't really believe what she's just heard. Like a drunk who's just been slapped in the face, she knows it's happened, and she knows it's supposed to hurt, but she's not really sure if it does or not.

'I don't know . . .' she mutters, stubbing out her cigarette and shakily lighting another one. 'I don't know . . .'

'It's all right, Mum,' I tell her. 'You don't have to –'

'It's so hard,' she says very quietly.

'I know.'

'I feel so . . .'

I wait, holding my breath, waiting for her to tell me how she feels . . . but it's just too much for her. She can't say any more. The words simply won't come out. Her mouth has tightened, her eyes have closed, her jaw is clenched, and all she can do is shake her head in suffered silence, trying to hold back the tears. And I know that

(it's her way of saying a prayer for me)

and I know that I hate myself for hearing a song in my head
when all I should be hearing is Mum's stifled sobs, but there's
nothing I can do about it. I can't do anything about the things
in my head. And even as I get up from the settee and go over
to Mum and hold her tightly in my arms, and her tears soak
into my skin, and her shaking soaks into my bones, and the
sound of 'Her Way of Praying' retreats into the inner silence
inside me, even then I can't stop hearing another song in my
head . . .

Another time.
Another Dawn.
Another song.

god help me (2)

A hymn.
   Dad's hymn.

have you been to jesus for the cleansing power?
are you washed in the blood of the lamb?
are you fully trusting in his grace this hour?
are you washed in the blood of the lamb?

are you washed in the blood?
in the soul-cleansing blood of the lamb?
are your garments spotless? are they white as snow?
are you washed in the blood of the lamb?

He plays it late at night when he's drunk out of his mind

are you walking by the saviour's side?
are you washed in the blood of the lamb?
do you rest each moment in the crucified?
are you washed in the blood of the lamb?

when he's drunk out of body and soul

when the bridegroom cometh will your robes be white?
pure and white in the blood of the lamb?
will your soul be ready for the mansions bright?
and be washed in the blood of the lamb?

when he's drunk himself out of himself

lay aside your garments that are stained with sin
and be washed in the blood of the lamb
there's a fountain flowing for the soul unclean
o be washed in the blood of the lamb

he weeps.

are you washed in the blood?
in the soul-cleansing blood of the lamb?
are your garments spotless? are they white as snow?
are you washed in the blood of the lamb?

God help me.

mushroom

I don't say anything to Mum as she sits there crying her heart out, I just hold her tear-soaked head in my arms and wish that things were different. I wish she wasn't crying. I wish I could stop listening to the storm in my head and the sound of the rain outside, and I wish I could do something to help Mum. But I can't.

And I hate myself for it.

It's so pathetic.

But I just can't find anything else. I can't find the right words. I can't find the right emotion. I can't concentrate. I can't think. Whatever's inside me, whatever I'm feeling... it feels like it belongs to someone else.

Another Dawn.

A sex thing.

A daughter.

Mum's crying so much now that at some point I start wondering how long a person can cry for. I mean, there must be a limit, mustn't there? You can't keep crying for ever. The tears have to dry up eventually.

But Mum doesn't seem to have any problem. She just

keeps on crying, sobbing, weeping, howling... and she doesn't stop until the doorbell suddenly rings, and Jesus and Mary leap off the settee and go running out into the hallway (*ROWROWROWROWROWROWROW*).

Mum straightens up and starts wiping tears and snot from her face.

'It's all right,' I tell her. 'We don't have to answer it.'

'No,' she sniffs, 'we'd better see who it is.'

'It doesn't matter, Mum. It's not –'

'Go on,' she insists. 'It might be important.'

We look at each other for a moment, and I realize what she means – i.e. that it might be someone about Dad – and although I don't think that's very likely, there's a part of me, a guilty part, that's secretly glad of the opportunity to do something other than hold Mum's head in my arms and listen to her cry. So, only half reluctantly, I go over to the front window and pull back the curtain to see who's at the door.

I'm not really thinking about who's going to be there – although, I suppose, in the back of my mind, I'm probably expecting it to be someone collecting for charity or something – and so, when I pull back the curtain and see two figures I recognize, it gives me a bit of a shock.

'Shit,' I mutter, blinking my eyes at Taylor and Mel.

Maybe if I'd been a bit quicker off the mark, maybe if I'd had the sense to close the curtain before they'd had a chance to see me, maybe everything might have been different.

But I wasn't.

And I didn't.

And it wasn't.

And in that split second between seeing Taylor and Mel

at the door, recognizing them, and beginning to think of closing the curtain, Taylor turns round, spots me at the window, and immediately starts shouting and gesticulating at me. I can't actually hear what she's saying (over the roar of the pouring rain), but from the look on her face and the way she's waving her hands about, I guess it's something like – 'Come *on*, open the fucking door, for Christ's sake! It's pissing down out here!'

'Who is it?' Mum asks.

'Taylor and Mel.'

'Who?'

I close the curtain and look at her. She's still sniffing and wiping her nose, but she's just about stopped crying now. Her face is red, her eyes bloodshot and swollen, and her cheeks are streaked with eyeliner and tears.

'Taylor and Mel,' I repeat. 'You know, the girls who came round last night? I'll tell them to go.'

'No,' Mum says. 'Don't be silly. I'm all right now.'

'Yeah, but I don't really –'

The dogs start yapping even louder as the doorbell rings again, and this time it doesn't stop. Taylor – or maybe it's Mel, but I'm pretty sure it's Taylor – is keeping her finger on the bell. So now the bell's ringing constantly, and Jesus and Mary are going mad (*ROWROWROWROWROWROWROW*), and the rain's hammering hard on the windows, and it's all so ridiculously noisy that Mum has to shout to be heard.

'GO ON, LOVE! LET THEM IN!'

'YEAH, BUT I DON'T –'

'YOU'D BETTER LET THEM IN!' she yells, forcing herself to smile. 'BEFORE THEY BREAK THE DOORBELL!'

about you (1)

Taylor doesn't wait for me to ask her in, she just barges her way into the hallway as soon as I open the front door, almost knocking me off my feet.

'Shit, it's cold,' she says, rubbing her hands together. 'What took you so long?'

Before I can answer, she bends down to say hello to Jesus and Mary, and I'm left looking at Mel behind her.

'Hey, Dawn,' she says, coming in and shutting the door. 'You all right?'

'Yeah . . .'

She's wearing pointy-toed black boots and a bright-pink parka with a fur-trimmed hood, and she's holding a carrier bag in her hand. From the size and shape of the carrier bag, I'm guessing it's filled with booze. Taylor's carrying a bag too, a biggish brown handbaggy kind of thing, like an expensive shoulder bag. She's wearing a short black puffy jacket, also with a fur-trimmed hood, and skin-tight jeans (I'm assuming, by the way, that Mel is wearing a very short skirt under her parka, because her legs are bare (and I can't help noticing, kind of embarrassingly, that they're also incredibly wondrous)).

'What going on?' I hear myself say.

'Nothing's *going on*,' Taylor replies, still making a fuss of the dogs. 'We just came round to say hello, that's all.'

I look down at her.

She smiles up at me. 'If that's all right with you?'

'Yeah, of course . . . I was just . . .'

She straightens up, standing too close to me. 'You were just what?'

I sigh. 'Nothing.'

'Good.' She grins at Mel, then turns back to me. 'You want to get us some glasses?'

Upstairs, in my room, after Taylor and Mel have taken their coats off (and I've found out that I was right about Mel's very short skirt), we adopt the same sitting positions as the night before: me at my desk, Taylor and Mel on the edge of the bed, Jesus and Mary stretched out behind them.

'Do you always do that?' Mel asks me.

'What?'

'The music,' she says, nodding at my PC. 'You put it on as soon as you sat down.'

'So?'

Mel shrugs. 'It's just the way you did it, you know . . . like it's some kind of . . . I don't know . . .'

'Nervous tic?' Taylor suggests, grinning at Mel.

I know she's just taking the piss, but the funny thing is (although it's not actually *funny*), she's probably not far from the truth. Putting on music, for me, *is* a kind of nervous tic. I do it without realizing I'm doing it. It's automatic. An involuntary and unconscious action. I come into my room, sit down at my desk, and the next thing I know I've logged on to my iTunes library, scrolled through the playlist, picked out 'About You', and hit the PLAY button.

(i can see
that you and me
live our lives in the pouring rain)

'What's all that?' says Mel, frowning as she looks across the room.

'What?'

'On the floor . . . under the window.'

My heart sinks a little as I realize what she's looking at. I mean, it doesn't *matter* . . . it's no big deal. It's just that earlier on, when I'd been thinking about how to kill God, and I'd come to the conclusion (or *a* conclusion) that I'd have to destroy all the Bibles in the world, and I'd realized that that was never going to happen . . . well, I'd just thought to myself – *OK, so it won't ever happen, but that doesn't mean I can't make a start, does it?* So I'd made a start by putting my two Bibles on a lightly paraffined baking tray, placing the baking tray on the floor under the window, and setting light to it.

The Bibles didn't burn all that well. I had to keep poking the pages around to keep the fire going, and even then I had to relight it about a million times. And despite having the window open, the smoke really stank up my room. But in the end I got what I wanted – two ex-Bibles, totally burned and totally unreadable.

Ashes to ashes.

Dust to dust.

And that's what Mel (and now Taylor) are looking at – a

pile of burned papers on a baking tray on the floor beneath the window.

'It's nothing,' I tell them. 'It's just... just some papers...'

'Papers?' asks Taylor, looking at me like I'm some kind of crazy-head. 'What kind of papers?'

'Just papers,' I shrug (and I know it's a pretty pathetic answer, but I really can't think of anything else to say).

Taylor stares at me for a moment, then she gives me one of those how-sad-are-you? looks – briefly closing her eyes and slowly shaking her head – and I feel kind of awkward and embarrassed, and I wonder why. Why the hell do I care what Taylor and Mel think of me? I've never cared what *any*one thinks of me before. I've always been perfectly content with my not-fitting-in-ness, my loser-ness, my sad-lumpy-weird-girl-ness.

Haven't I?

'Yeah, anyway,' says Taylor, dipping into Mel's carrier bag. 'Who wants a drink?'

She pulls out a bottle of vodka, uncaps it, and takes a swig. 'Where's the glasses?' she says, looking around.

Mel passes her two of the three half-pint glasses that I brought up from the kitchen (and I'm still wondering why they insisted on three, when I *told* them that I didn't need one), and Taylor pours a couple of inches of vodka into each of the glasses and passes one to Mel.

As Mel takes a drink from her glass, I suddenly realize that I'm hyper-overly aware of myself – sitting here watching them, looking at them, studying them. They're both sitting there on my bed in their skinny-tight-short-skirted-flashy-fleshed girli-ness, slugging neat vodka from half-pint glasses... and it all seems so detached from me – like it's here, but it's not here. It's a hundred million miles away. But it's also incredibly close. In fact, it's so close, so very very close to me, that it's gone beyond my eyes and I'm seeing it inside my head like a scarily magnified dream.

I'm seeing every tiny aspect of Taylor's face – her perfect cheekbones, her sculpted eyebrows, her pink-painted lips. I'm seeing the smooth skin of her shoulders, pale and muscled under a black halterneck top . . . and the way she's holding her cigarette, her red-varnished fingernails gleaming like claws in the smoke-ribboned light. I'm seeing the faint remains of a telephone number written in black biro on the back of her hand. I'm seeing the star-like pores of her skin in the blackness.

And (somehow) at the same time, I'm seeing everything about Mel – every single stitch of her tight Killah vest and the shapes beneath it and the weightless shimmer of her almost-see-through black net miniskirt and her deep dark eyes and warm olive skin . . . but it's doing so much to me that I can't bear to look.

I can't . . .

I won't . . .

> *(i know there's something good*
> *about you*
> *about you)*

No, I can't feel anything like that.

'You want some?' Taylor says to me.

'What?'

'Vodka,' she says (and I'm outside my head again now, I can see her brandishing the bottle at me). 'You want some?'

'No, thanks.'

'You sure?'

'Yeah.'

'Have some of this then,' she says, pulling another bottle out of the carrier bag.

It's a silver-coloured bottle with a black neck and red writing on the side. There's writing on the neck as well, but the shrink-wrapped plasticky stuff is a bit scraped off so I can't make out what it says.

'What is it?' I ask Taylor, angling my head to try to read the writing on the side of the bottle.

'It's called Revolver,' she tells me as she pours some into a glass. 'Don't worry, there's no alcohol in it.' She smiles mockingly at me, as if disliking alcohol is *the* most puerile thing in the world, and she gets up off the bed and brings the drink over to me.

I look up at her, standing in front of me, offering me the glass.

'Go on,' she sneers. 'Take it. It's rude to refuse a drink.'

I look at the glass. It's filled to the brim with something that looks remarkably like Coke. Same colour, same fizziness, same overall Coke-iness.

'What's in it?' I ask.

'Christ,' Taylor snaps. 'I don't *know* . . . it's just one of those energy drinks, you know, like Red Bull or something.' She shoves the glass at me. 'It's just a fucking drink, all right? I mean, shit, I'm just trying to be fucking *friendly* here –'

'Caffeine, ginseng and taurine,' Mel says from the bed.

I look over to see her reading from the back of the bottle.

'And guarana and fruit juice,' she adds, looking up. 'That's it. Fruit juice, caffeine, ginseng, guarana and taurine.'

'Taurine?' I say, taking the drink from Taylor.

'Yeah,' says Mel. 'It's a natural stimulant. You get it in Boost bars.' She smiles at me. 'That's why they're called *Boost* bars.'

'That's guarana,' I tell her.

'What?'

'Guarana. Boost bars have got guarana in them. Not taurine.' I look at Mel. 'It's the same *kind* of stuff as taurine –'

'Yeah, ycah, yeah,' says Taylor, pretending to yawn as she sits back down on the bed. 'Fascinating.'

'It makes you late,' I say, and I'm surprised to find myself staring at her.

She looks hard at me. '*What?*'

'Guarana,' I say. 'It makes you late for school.'

She gives me another one of those looks. 'Yeah?'

I nod (thinking of my Invisible Coat, and how that makes me late for things too, and thinking of that makes me smile). 'Yeah,' I say (not really knowing what I'm doing, but not really caring either). 'You see, what happens is – you wake up in the morning feeling really tired, so you take a shower, and you wash yourself with a shower gel that's got guarana in it . . . you know, because it's supposed to give you an instant energy surge and transform the way you feel.' (I'm remembering this word for word from the shower-gel bottle, by the way.) 'And you think that's it, you're exhilarated now, you can get dressed and get off to school, *no* problem. And then you quickly wash your hair, but by mistake you use a herbal shampoo with mimosa in it, which is *known* to aid tranquillity and leave you calm and relaxed after a long and stressful day –'

'Dawn?' says Mel, interrupting me. 'What the *fuck* are you talking about?'

'Well,' I tell her. 'You have to wash yourself again, don't you? I mean, you've zapped yourself up with the guarana shower gel, but *then* you've gone and undone the zappiness with the relaxing mimosa shampoo. So you have to start washing again with the guarana shower gel to re-wake yourself up.'

'Right,' says Mel. 'And that's why it makes you late for school?'

'Exactly.'

'Shit,' Taylor says to Mel, shaking her head. 'If she's like this *before* she's drunk anything with caffeine in it, imagine what she's going to be like *after* she drinks it.'

I look at the drink in my hand.

It's stopped bubbling.

I raise the glass to my lips and take a sip.

It tastes OK. Sweet and sugary. Kind of fruity, but not *specifically* fruity. I mean, it doesn't have the taste of any fruit in particular, it's just *generally* fruity. A bit like Red Bull, I suppose (like Taylor said). Which is OK.

'All right?' asks Taylor.

'Yeah, not bad.'

'Good.' She raises her glass. 'Cheers then.'

And she drinks her vodka, and Mel drinks hers, and they both smile at me (Mel a little sadly) as I raise my glass again and drink it all down in one.

When I put the empty glass on the desk and turn back to

Taylor and Mel, I see Jesus sitting up on the bed behind them, his head held still, his small eyes fixed on mine, and just for a moment – a seemingly infinite moment – it's another time, another Dawn, another Jesus . . .

Another time.

(Jesus was sitting up then, just as he is now, with the very same look in his dog-brown eyes (*i can't help you*) and I felt so sorry for him. Because dogs don't *know* things, they don't understand things, they don't know *why* anything is anything. All they know is good and bad and happy and sad. And Jesus knew it was bad, but I didn't want him to feel bad for me. And as the song played on

(are you washed in the blood of the lamb?)

I heard a trembling voice saying, 'It's all right, Jesus. It's all right.')

'Right then,' says Taylor, grinning wildly and clapping her hands together (like the party has just begun). 'Who's up for some extreme makeovering?'

I'm not quite *there* just now, I'm still a bit mesmerized by the echoes of Jesus's eyes, so I can't really say anything, or take anything in, but as Jesus lowers himself down to the bed, his eyes still fixed on mine, I'm peripherally aware of Taylor unzipping her shoulder bag and taking out a couple of carrier bags full of stuff.

i can't help you

125

'I know,' I tell Jesus now. 'It's all right.'

'What's all right?' asks Taylor.

look at her, watch her

I look at Taylor. 'What?'

She frowns at me. 'Who're you talking to?'

'What?'

'Who are you *talking* to?'

'When?'

'Now . . . just then . . .'

I give her an innocent look – like, what are you *talking* about? who do you *think* I'm talking to? – and I say to her, 'I'm talking to you.'

She stares at me.

I smile at her, not knowing why. 'What have you got there?' I ask, glancing at the carrier bags she took out of her shoulder bag.

She hesitates for a moment, still as puzzled by my behaviour as I am, then she shakes her head, dismissing it from her mind, and starts showing me what's in the carrier bags. 'This,' she says, 'is for you.'

I watch as she upends one of the bags and empties the contents onto the bed. It's clothing. Girl's clothing. And now I'm the one looking puzzled.

'What is it?' I ask.

As Mel picks up a very-small-looking bright-pink T-shirt and holds it up for me to see, Taylor says to me, 'What do you think? D'you like it?'

The words ROCK 'N' ROLL STAR are spelled out in sequins on the front of the shirt.

'What is it?' I repeat.

'It's your new look,' Taylor says. Then, to Mel, 'Show her the skirt.'

Mel holds up a short denim skirt, waggling it from side to side.

'You'll look great in it,' Taylor says, grinning at me. 'Hot stuff.'

'I don't get it,' I say. 'What do you mean?'

'We're giving you a makeover,' she tells me, digging into the other carrier bag. 'A whole new look.' She takes a load of stuff from the bag and dumps it on the bed. Bottles, sprays, a make-up bag. 'See?' she says. 'New clothes, new hair, a new face . . .' She laughs. 'You'll be a brand new Dawn.'

'Why?' I mutter, looking from Taylor to Mel. 'I mean . . . why?'

'It's just what you need,' Taylor says, getting to her feet. 'It'll perk you right up. Make you feel good about yourself.'

'Yeah, but —'

'We thought you were a bit down,' Mel says to me. 'You know, yesterday . . . you seemed kind of miserable.'

'Pissed off,' Taylor adds.

'About your dad and everything.'

'Yeah,' says Taylor, coming across to me with the bottle of Revolver in her hand. 'So we thought we'd cheer you up. Here, have some more.' She picks up my empty glass, fills it, and hands it to me.

I take it from her.

'Drink it,' she says.

I drink it.

'Right,' she says, smiling wickedly. 'We're going to pimp your ass, girl.'

happy when it rains (2)

Q. Why do you let people do things to you that you don't
want them to do? Why can't you just tell them – *no, I
don't want you to do that*? I mean, what *is* it that stops
you from making a stand? Is it fear? The fear of being
ridiculed? The fear of conflict? The fear of being disliked?
Or is it simply a weakness? A flaw in your character, a lack
of self-confidence, an absence of courage?
Why are you so meek?
A. I don't know. I don't know why I let these things
happen.

But maybe I just think that sometimes, like now (as the guitars
ring out and the drums beat hard and Taylor and Mel smoke
their cigarettes and drink their vodka and talk and laugh and
move to the music around me) . . . maybe I just think that
letting it happen is the easiest way out.
Easier than saying no.
And, besides, it's not *that* hard to just sit here on the bed,
drinking this fruity-flavoured fizzy drink, getting into the
music while Taylor and Mel fuss about with my hair and my
face. In fact, it kind of feels OK.

'Keep still,' Taylor tells me.

She's doing something to my eyes – brushing some stuff on them, making them up (she's already lipsticked my lips and put some stuff on my cheeks). Mel is behind me, crouched down on the bed, fiddling around with my hair. I don't know what she's doing, but it feels quite nice. And I can see her reflection in the mirror on the opposite wall, and she looks like she's enjoying herself, and that makes me feel kind of all right too.

It's still raining hard outside, and it sounds cold and nasty, and I'm glad I'm in here, in the rainless comfort of my room. I have a nice warm feeling in my belly.

'You should do this all the time,' Mel says.

'Do what?'

'Look after yourself.' She runs a brush through my hair. 'All it takes is a little bit of effort, and it makes so much difference. You'd be amazed how much better you feel when you look nice.'

I start to shake my head.

'Will you keep *still*?' Taylor snaps at me.

'Sorry.' I look in the mirror at Mel. 'It's a waste of time.'

'What is?'

'Trying to make myself look nice – it's pointless.'

'Why?'

'You *know* why. I mean, look at me . . .' I look distastefully at my reflection in the mirror, and despite my newly modelled hair and my lippied-up lips and my (frankly) quite delectable-looking eyes (which I have to admit look pretty stunning), I can still only see myself for what I am – a round-shouldered lump in baggy black clothes. Round head, dumpyish legs, dumpyish arms, lumpyish lumps . . .

That's me, that is.

That's me.

'Don't put yourself down,' Mel says.

'I'm not –'

'Yeah, you are. I mean, all right, so you're not exactly Kylie Minogue, but you've still got a lot going for you.'

'Yeah?' I laugh. 'Like what?'

She sits back and studies me in the mirror. 'You've got a pretty face, nice eyes, your skin's OK . . .'

'Yeah,' Taylor agrees, still concentrating on my eyes. 'Her skin's surprisingly good, actually.'

'Same as her hair,' says Mel. 'All it needs is a decent cut.' She smiles at me. 'And as for the rest of you . . .'

'Yeah, right,' I say. 'The rest of me. Exactly.'

'What do you mean?' says Mel.

'What do you *think* I mean?'

'She thinks she's fat,' Taylor says matter-of-factly to Mel.

Mel scowls at me. 'You're not *fat*, for Christ's sake.'

'No?

'No.'

'Yeah, well, I'm not *skinny*, am I?'

'So what? Just because you're not skinny doesn't mean you're fat. I mean, look at you . . .' She puts her hands on my shoulders and gently pulls me back, so I'm sitting up straight, then she runs her hands down my back, kind of gathering up the cloth of my baggy old Jesus and Mary Chain T-shirt as she goes, so it tightens against my body. 'There,' she says, looking (almost triumphantly) at me in the mirror. 'See? I mean, look at those curves . . . I know girls who'd *die* for a body like that. You've just got to stop hiding it away, that's all.'

As I stare at myself in the mirror, studying the shape of my body – the roundness of my belly, the unfamiliar outline of my breasts – I can't help questioning everything. I mean, curves? Is that really what they are? Or am I being taken for a ride here? Are Taylor and Mel just taking the piss? Suckering me with their sweet words and their fake flattery? Making me think that I don't look as bad as I think?

Q. Why would they do that?
A. Why would they not?

But if that's what they *are* doing, if they really *are* just taking the piss, then:

Q. How come you're feeling OK? I mean, how come you're actually *enjoying* this? How come you *like* sitting here, looking at yourself in the mirror, while Mel sits behind you pulling your T-shirt tight?
A. I don't know. I don't know why I'm feeling OK.

But maybe it's just that sometimes, like now (as the guitars ring out and the drums beat hard and Mel lets go of my T-shirt and Taylor stands up and lights another cigarette and refills my glass) . . . maybe, sometimes, I just *need* to feel OK.

And I do.

But then Taylor hands me the drink and says, 'OK, get that down your neck and then get your clothes off,' and as she stands there grinning down at me, the world seems to stop for a moment (at least, *my* world seems to stop), and suddenly I don't feel quite so OK any more, and all I can do is stare back up at Taylor, my eyes unblinking and my mouth hanging open in stunned disbelief.

Am I imagining things?

Or did she *really* just tell me to take off my clothes?

'It's all right,' Mel says, laughing quietly at the look on my face. 'Don't look so worried.' She scoops up the pink T-shirt and the denim skirt and drops them into my lap. 'Go on,' she says. 'Try them on.'

I glance down for a moment, staring stupidly at the flimsy clothes, then I look up at Taylor. She's smirking at me, enjoying my embarrassment, and I know there's nothing for me to be embarrassed about . . . I mean, it's not as if I misunderstood or misinterpreted her when she told me to take my clothes off. I didn't jump to the wrong conclusion or anything. All I did was get confused. And Taylor knows that, and she knows that I know it. And that makes me feel even more embarrassed.

'What's the matter?' she asks innocently.

'Nothing,' I tell her (with as much *un*embarrassment as I can manage).

She smirks again. 'Right.'

For want of anything better to do, I take a fairly big gulp of my drink. It tastes kind of different now – a bit less fruity, maybe, a bit more . . . I don't know. A bit more something-elsey. And I'm tempted to say something – like, *Is this the same stuff I was drinking before?* – but Taylor is still looking down at me (literally *and* figuratively), and I don't want to give her anything else to sneer about. And I'm probably just being over-sensitive to the taste of the drink anyway – my taste buds hyped up with embarrassmentized adrenalin. So

I don't say anything, I just swallow the drink and stare at the clothes in my lap.

They're far too small for me.

They look like something a Bratz doll would wear.

'Go on then,' says Taylor, jutting her chin at the clothes. 'What are you waiting for?'

I shake my head. 'I don't think they'll fit me.'

'Yeah, they will,' Mel says. 'They're just a bit closer-fitting than the stuff you usually wear, that's all.'

Taylor laughs. 'A *bit* closer-fitting?' She reaches down and tugs dismissively at the front of my T-shirt. 'I mean, shit, a *tent's* closer-fitting than this.'

'It's *supposed* to be baggy,' I protest.

'That's not *baggy*,' she says. 'That's *sacky*. And these...' She flicks her hand at my faded old combat pants. 'These are the fattest pants I've ever *seen*. They'd look big on Biggie Smalls.' She shakes her head. 'Who the fuck's going to want to find out what you've got in there?'

'I don't *want* anyone to find out what I've got in there,' I tell her. 'I wear these because *I* like them. They're comfortable –'

'*Comfortable?*' Taylor sneers. 'Clothes aren't meant to be *comfortable*. They're not fucking armchairs.'

'Yeah, well...' I say.

And I'm kind of annoyed with myself now, because I sound so *sulky*, as if all this stupidity really bothers me. Which it doesn't, of course.

Of course.

'Come on, Dawn,' Mel says, smiling at me as she scooches round and sits down next to me. 'Just give it a go. Try the clothes on. You'll look great in them.'

I drink some more of my slightly-odd-but-actually-quite-nice-tasting drink. 'I don't *want* to look great,' I tell her.

'Yeah, you do. Everyone wants to look great.' She puts her hand on my knee. 'I mean, we all want to be *looked* at, don't we?'

I stare at her hand.

It's small, smaller than I would have imagined (if, that is, I'd ever imagined the size of her hand, which I haven't).

She has badly chewed fingernails.

A plain silver ring on her middle finger.

She has faded white scars on her forearm.

'Look,' says Taylor (a bit less sneery now). 'We're just trying to help you out here. I mean, the thing is, if you carry on dressing like you do . . . you know, like some dowdy old bag lady, the only interest you're ever going to get is from desperate boys with white sticks and guide dogs.' She grins at me. 'Is that what you want?'

I grin back at her, suddenly feeling surprisingly OK again. 'I went out with a blind boy once,' I tell her. 'He was all right, actually. Until he dumped me.'

Taylor looks a bit stunned. 'You got dumped by a *blind* guy?'

'Yeah . . . but it was my fault, really. I stole his dog.'

'You *what*?'

'I stole his guide dog.'

'Why?'

'Well, it was a really nice dog – a black German shepherd – and I really wanted it. And this guy was blind, you know . . .? I mean, what's a blind guy going to do if you steal his dog? It's not like he can go out looking for it, is it?'

'So you actually *stole* his dog?' Mel says.

'Yeah.'

'What did he do?'

'Who – the dog?'

'No, the blind guy.'

'He sent his mum round to my house, and she took the dog back.' I shrug. 'I *told* her I was only borrowing it for a while, but I don't think she believed me.'

'And that's why he dumped you?' asks Taylor. 'Because you stole his guide dog?'

'Yeah.'

Mel looks at me. 'Really?'

'Yeah.'

'That *really* happened?'

I look back at her for a moment, smiling at the bemusement on her face, and then I shake my head and say, 'No, it didn't really happen. I just made it up.'

'You think that's funny?' Taylor says to me.

I shrug again. 'Not really.'

She shakes her head. 'I don't *get* you.'

'There's nothing to get.'

'No?'

We look at each other.

She lights a cigarette, sips her vodka.

I take a drink from my glass.

And she says, 'Maybe you don't *want* guys looking at you.'

'I don't really care –'

'Maybe the rumours are true.'

'What rumours?'

'You know... the names they call you at school. Dyke, lesbo, todger-dodger –'

'I've never heard that one.'

She smiles at me. 'I'm not having a go at you, you know... I'm not *judging* you or anything. I mean, me and Mel don't give a fuck *what* you are.' She grins at Mel. 'Do we, darling?'

'No,' says Mel, smiling at me. 'We're *very* open-minded.'

There's a moment's silence then, a strange little moment in which we all just look at each other, and there's a fleeting sense of genuine (and totally *non*-sexual) intimacy between us, and it feels so good that, just for a second, we all let out little breaths of quiet amusement.

And, with that, the moment's over.

But, still, it happened.

And what's happened can't be unhappened.

'So,' says Taylor, puffing (slightly self-consciously) on her cigarette. 'Are you going to try these clothes on, or what?'

I sigh, already knowing what I'm going to say, because letting it happen *is* the easiest way out, it *is* easier than saying no, and besides...

There is no besides.

I look at Mel, and she says, 'What's the matter? Are you all right?'

'What?'

'Are you OK?'

'Yeah... yeah, I'm fine.' I smile at her. 'I'm shy.'

'Sorry?'

'You'll have to leave the room. If you want me to try the clothes on, I mean. I don't like getting undressed in front of other people.'

'What's the matter?' says Taylor, grinning at me. 'Do you think we're going to go crazy with lust at the sight of your naked body?'

I look at her, and for a second or two I can't seem to focus my eyes. I close them, open them again, then I try just closing one. And that does the trick. I can see her quite clearly now.

'What?' I say to her.

She shakes her head. 'I said, do you think we're going to go crazy –'

'Come on, Tay,' Mel says, getting to her feet. 'Give the girl some privacy, for Christ's sake. Let her get changed in peace.' She jerks her head at the door. 'Come on, I need a piss anyway.'

'Oh, yeah . . .' Taylor says. 'Right.'

And as the two of them head for the door, I'm wondering if it's just me (in my state of unfocusedness), or was the tone of Taylor's voice – *Oh, yeah . . . right* – was that the tone of someone who's just been given a conspiratorial wink?

'Five minutes all right?' Taylor asks me.

'Sorry?'

'Is five minutes long enough for you to get changed?'

'Yeah . . . yeah, fine.' I look at her. 'You're just going to the toilet, yeah?'

'Yeah.' She gives me a look. 'Is that a problem?'

'No, of course not . . .'

Which, strictly speaking, is the truth. I *don't* have a problem with them going to the toilet. But what I *do* have a problem with is the idea of them talking to Mum. I don't want them to talk to her. But if I tell them not to, they'll probably think that:

1) I'm ashamed of them

or 2) I'm ashamed of Mum.

And I don't want them to think either of those things. Because they're not true.

I just don't want them to talk to Mum because...

Just because.

'See you in a minute then,' Taylor says.

She goes out, followed by Mel, and a few seconds later Jesus and Mary hop off the bed and follow them down the stairs. I wonder for a moment if I ought to call out after Taylor and Mel – 'My mum's not feeling too good at the moment, so it's probably best if you don't disturb her.' But by the time I've thought about it, they're already downstairs, and they probably wouldn't have taken any notice of me anyway...

So now I'm on my own, staring at a whore-faced Dawn Bundy in the mirror, and for a second or two there's a strangely awkward silence between us. It's the kind of silence you get when you're alone with yourself and you suddenly become intensely aware of the fact that you are *you*. You are the only conscious entity in the world. You are that awful thing in the mirror.

A sex thing.

A girl.

You are Dawn Bundy.

god help me (3)

My name is Dawn Bundy.

I'm thirteen years old.

My name is Dawn Bundy.

I don't want to drink anything, Dad. Please don't make me. I don't like the taste of it. I don't like what it does to you. I don't want you to be like this – drunk out of your mind, out of body and soul, playing your scary hymn over and over again. Please, Dad, don't cry.

I don't want you to cry.

I can't take it any more.

So, yes, I'll take this glass from your trembling hand and I'll drink what you want me to drink, because letting it happen is the easiest way out.

God help me.

head (2)

I have to turn my back on the Dawn Bundy in the mirror as I get up off the bed and start clambering out of my Biggie-Smalls-sized pants, because whoever that Dawn Bundy is (the one in the mirror) and whatever she thinks she's doing, I don't want to see her watching me. I don't want to be aware of her judgemental looks as I stumble around like a gigantic idiot, trying to get my trousers off without falling over. I don't want to see her shaking her head at me, saying – 'What the hell do you think you're *doing*?' – as I begin squeezing myself into a ridiculously short denim skirt.

I don't want to see myself in her eyes.

I don't want to be me.

I can't face it.

> *(i walk away*
> *from your head)*

The skirt, surprisingly, doesn't take all that much effort to get on. It's a bit of a struggle getting it up and over my thighs, but once that's done . . . well, it's actually not a bad fit. I mean, it's tight – a lot tighter than I'm used to – and it definitely doesn't need the little belt that goes with it to stay up, but it's not *painfully* tight or anything. It's not cutting into my skin. And, even more surprisingly, it kind of looks (and feels) pretty good. Admittedly, I'm still not facing the mirror, so I'm only seeing things from above, so I'm probably not seeing the full-on reality of my pudgy white legs in a very short and very tight skirt, but even so . . .

I can't help smiling.

It's a funny-feeling smile though. Kind of loose, like my lips are drooping. And maybe my tongue's hanging out a bit too. And my teeth feel too big.

'Christ,' I hear myself say.

And my voice is a little bit slurred.

And I realize that I'm just standing here, staring down at the floor, and everything seems to be moving – my head, the floor, the walls, the music . . .

And I think . . .

What's the use?

I don't want to think. I just want to do this, whatever this is. I just want to let it happen. And so that's what I'm doing – letting it happen. I'm doing this thing. I'm standing with my back to the mirror, stripping off my baggy old T-shirt, and I'm just starting to pull the very small bright-pink T-shirt over my head when the bedroom door suddenly swings open and Mel comes breezing back in.

'Hey, look at *you*,' she says, smiling broadly.

And all at once I'm petrified, panicking, my heart beating like crazy, because Mel can *see* me. She can see my semi-nakedness. And I don't want that. I can't bear it. It kills me. So I have to turn away, hiding myself from her eyes, and I have to try covering my body with one arm while desperately trying to pull down the T-shirt at the same time . . .

'Are you all right?' Mel says, confused. 'What's the matter?'

'Nothing,' I mumble, struggling with the T-shirt. 'I just . . . I'm just trying to get this on –'

'Here,' she says, moving towards me. 'Let me help you.'

'No . . .' I start to say, turning away even more.

'Don't be stupid,' she sighs, reaching out and putting her hand on my back. 'It's all right –'

'*NO!*'

The scream comes out of me as her hand touches my skin. I can't help it. Her hand is ice-cold, red-hot . . . a million-volt electric shock. It crashes right through me, jolting me across the room, and as I cower against the wall, whimpering like a baby, it's all I can do to stay on my feet.

'Dawn?' Mel whispers fearfully. 'What's the –?'

'*Don't touch me!*' I hear myself hiss at her through gritted teeth.

'I was only –'

'*DON'T!*'

'Yeah, all right,' she mutters. 'OK . . .'

I can sense her backing away from me now, and I don't have to see her face to know that she's staring at me in wide-eyed horror. I'm a panic-stricken crazy thing, a screaming lunatic cringing pathetically against the wall, a fat-faced maniac fighting her way into a miniature pink T-shirt . . .

Horror is the only reaction I deserve.

(the beat of your heart
your cold empty heart)

I've just about got the T-shirt on now. And although there's not very much of it, so it doesn't really cover up all that much of me (in fact, it leaves more of me uncovered than covered), there's still something about it – the feel of the cloth on my skin – that gives me a renewed sense of semi-security. I'm *dressed* now. My arms might be bare, my belly showing . . . and there's an unfamiliar (and slightly unsettling) amount of cleavage looking up at me. But at least I'm dressed. And somehow that makes me feel safer.

It allows me to start breathing normally again.

It stops my head spinning so much.

It calms the terror in my heart.

'I'm sorry, Dawn,' Mel says quietly. 'I didn't mean –'

'No, it's all right,' I tell her, straightening myself up. 'It's my fault . . . it's just . . .'

I take a deep breath, letting it out slowly, and I force myself to turn round and look at Mel. And what I see is kind of surprising. I mean, yes, there is *some* horror in her eyes, as I knew there would be, but it's nowhere near as bad as I thought. In fact, it's so faint that if I wasn't looking for it, I'm not even sure that I'd see it. What I would see, though (and what I can see), is something that looks like concern.

'Sorry,' I tell her, trying to smile. 'I mean, I'm sorry if I frightened you . . . it's just –'

'It's OK,' she says, smiling back at me. 'You don't have to explain.'

I shake my head. 'It's just that I get a bit . . . I don't know. I'm a bit funny about things, I suppose . . .'

'It's all right,' Mel tells me. 'I understand.'

'Do you?'

'Yeah, I think so.'

We share another one of those moments then – a silent pause, both of us looking at each other, not sure what to say, or if anything needs to be said – and just for a second or two everything seems OK. My head is clear, the floor isn't moving any more, the music is darkly sweet and perfect

(hey hey hey
want you to stay)

and then Jesus and Mary come trotting in through the door, soaking wet from the rain, and they both shake themselves (as ineffectually as ever), and Mel starts laughing at them, and then she stops laughing and looks up as Taylor strolls in.

And she takes one look at me and says, 'Wow! Who's the babe?'

And that's kind of it, really.

The floor starts moving again, circling around my feet, and my head starts circling with it, and everything else – the room, the walls, the window, the ceiling . . . the air, the world, the bubble I live in – everything seems to slowly dissolve into a whirling-swirling-circling blur of voices and music and movement and time.

I remember some of it.

I remember Taylor walking all around me, circling me, looking me up and down, nodding her head and smiling her approval at me – 'Look at you . . . you look *stunning*!' – like I'm some kind of unbelievable miracle or something. And I know she's just screwing me around, but I don't care. Because I'm looking at myself in the mirror now and I'm actually liking what I see. I know it's not me, of course. I know it's only a painted face and a non-delectable body squeezed into a short denim skirt and a bright-pink T-shirt (with *ROCK 'N' ROLL STAR* spelled out in sequins on the front), but it's something that has a discernible *shape*. A womanly, girly, and (at a pinch) curvy shape.

And I like it.

I like it too when Taylor pours us all a drink and raises her glass to me and says, 'Cheers, hot stuff!'

And Mel smiles at me and says, 'Cheers!'

And they both down their drinks in one.

And it'd be rude of me not to do the same, so I glug my drink down too – and immediately start coughing and gagging. Because it doesn't taste fruity any more. It tastes like liquid heat.

'Christ!' I gasp, trying to get some air into my lungs. 'What the hell –?'

'You need a bra,' Taylor says.

'Uh?'

'A decent bra,' she says, coming over to me, her eyes fixed on my chest. 'I mean, where the hell d'you get that thing you're wearing – Oxfam?'

I look down at myself and realize that my bra is visible beneath the flimsy T-shirt. 'What's wrong with it?' I ask.

'Everything,' Taylor says. 'It's too big for you, for a start. It's completely the wrong size. And it's *ancient* . . . I mean, look at it . . .' She reaches out and fingers the strap. I flinch away. 'It's got nothing *to* it,' she goes on. 'You need something that makes the most of what you've got. This old rag doesn't do anything for you.' She smiles at me 'It's got no *oomph*.'

'It's my mum's,' I mutter.

'What?'

'It's my mum's bra –'

'Your *mum's*?'

'Yeah. All mine are –'

'Jesus! You're wearing your mum's *bra*?'

'All mine are in the wash.'

'Shit!' she says, shaking her head in disgust. 'I don't believe it. You've got all this money and you're still wearing your mum's fucking bra –'

'What money?'

'What?'

'What money?' I repeat.

She stares at me for a moment, her eyes blank, and then – with a curious sense of false bravado – she lights a cigarette and blows out smoke. 'All this,' she says, waving her hand round the room, indicating all my stuff. 'I mean, you can afford all this, but you can't afford to get yourself some decent bras . . . that's all I'm saying.' She smiles at me. 'It's money well spent, Dawn. Honestly, you'd be amazed . . . I mean, look at me.' She straightens her back and puffs out her chest at me. I don't *want* to look, but I can't see any way out of it. So I glance down at her chest, and I see two perfect breasts nestling perfectly in her black halterneck top.

'It's a Secret Embrace,' Taylor says proudly. 'Pushes you up, makes your tits look great.' She starts undoing her top. 'You want to see it? You can try it on if you want. It's probably a bit small for you . . .'

And before I know what's happening, Taylor's standing there, right in front of me, showing off her sexy black bra, all sleek and lacy and smooth, and all at once I'm petrified again, panicking, my heart beating like crazy, because I can *see* her. I can see her semi-nakedness. And I don't know if I like it or not. I don't know if I can bear it. So I have to look away, hiding my eyes from her, and I have to try not to feel scarily mixed up about everything . . .

'What's the matter with her?' Taylor asks Mel. 'What's she doing?'

'It's all right,' Mel tells her quietly. 'Just do up your shirt.'

'Why? I was only showing her –'

'Just do it, Tay.'

I remember that.

And drinking some more.

And starting to feel OK again.

And talking about stuff – school, clothes, music, places, TV, gossip, people, secrets – most of which I don't really care about or don't understand or don't even listen to, but it's OK. It's just talking. Just talking. That's all. We're just talking. And the rain is still beating down outside, and the music is still playing

(off your head
off your head
hanging from your head)

and I don't know what time it is now but it feels pretty late, and I'm feeling all right, I'm feeling all wrong, I'm feeling like another Dawn in another time . . . another Dawn, a sex thing, a daughter, a thing in a cave inside my head where it's cold and it's dark and there is no sound (*are you washed in the blood?*) and there is no sound and I try to make the cave soft like a pillow but most of the time it's hard like stone to keep out the monsters (*was he up to something?*) but I don't care any more. I don't care about anything any more because I'm not here any more I'm not here I'm not here I'm not here I'm not here I'm not listening (*who?*) I'm not saying anything I'm going out of my mind (*god help me*) I'm out of my mind (*your dad*) I'm out of his body and soul and I'm not listening (*your dad – was he up to something?*) no no no no no . . .

No.

There is no <u>Reason Four</u>.

My dad . . .

No.

bleed me

My name is Dawn Bundy.
  I'm thirteen years old.
  My name is Dawn Bundy.

It's a cold December night two years ago, and I'm lying in
my bed, wrapped up tightly in my old white dressing gown,
and Jesus and Mary are trembling and shaking on the bed
beside me. They're frightened. And I'm frightened too.
Because Dad's downstairs, drunk out of his mind, wailing
and moaning and singing along to his awful hymn

  (are you washed in the blood of the lamb?)

and it sounds like madness.
  I've never been afraid of my dad before, no matter what
state he's been in, because whatever state he's been in, he's
always been my dad, and he's always been himself, and we've
always loved each other.
  But I'm afraid of him now.
  Because he *isn't* himself now. He *isn't* my dad. He's

149

become someone else, some*thing* else . . . I can hear it in his lunatic howling. I can feel it, sense it. I *know* it.

He's finally given in to his demons.

(are you fully trusting in his grace this hour?)

No.

My name is Dawn Bundy.

I'm thirteen years old.

I'm scared to death.

There's no one else here. Mum is out somewhere. With friends, at a party, a nightclub . . . I don't know. She had an argument with Dad. She went out. She's not here. She can't help me.

Downstairs, a glass smashes.

Jesus whimpers.

Mary shivers.

'It's all right,' I whisper to them. 'It's all right.'

It's not all right.

It never will be.

The hymn is still playing when Dad comes into my room. The music gets louder for a moment as the door slowly opens

(when the bridegroom cometh will your robes be white?)

and then it quietens again.

'Dawn?'

His voice is dark, unfamiliar.

I pretend I'm asleep.

Unsteady footsteps shuffle across the room.

'Dawn? Are you awake?'

He can hardly speak. His words come out as: *Dorr . . . ? Uuway?*

I hear him stumble, cracking his shin on the bed.

'Shit.'

I hear Jesus growl at him, a frightened snarl.

'Go on,' Dad slurs at him. 'Off the bed . . . both of you.'

I feel him sweeping his arm at Jesus and Mary, clumsily (but not aggressively) moving them off the bed. I feel them hopping off. I feel him sitting down heavily on the edge of the bed. I hear him take a drink of something.

And then he sighs, 'God help me.'

And I can smell the terrible drink-smell of his breath.

'Dawn?' he says again. And this time he nudges me with his hand. 'Come on, Dawn, please wake up. I've been praying for you.'

He says other things to me too – sickeningly absurd things about Jesus the Saviour, Jesus the Crucified . . . and he talks to me about love and sin and faith and God – and he cries and he moans, and he begs me to take a drink from his glass . . . and then the world stops moving.

Everything is moveless and dead.

And I'm not Dawn any more. I'm just a frozen thing, lying perfectly still, making my body as hard as stone, trying to not feel what happens . . .

But I feel it.

I can't say any more. I can't live it. I can't remember it.
It hurts.
It makes me bleed.
It makes me cry.

Afterwards, when I'm lying pained and bloodied in my bed (and I'm already beginning to crawl into my cave), all I'm aware of is the sound of Dad weeping as he sways and stumbles towards the door.
The hymn has stopped playing.
The house is unnaturally quiet.
My heart is dead.
'God, forgive me,' I hear Dad sob as he opens the door and leaves. 'Oh God . . . please forgive me.'

darklands (2)

He only did it to me once. That one time, on that cold December night two years ago, two weeks before he walked out of the house and never came back... that was it.
The only time.

(and i awake from dreams
to a scary world of screams)

And there really is no <u>Reason Four</u>. Yes, I want to kill God for making my dad lose himself, and for turning him into something else, but I *don't* blame God for making my dad do what he did to me, because I don't think God made him do it. I don't *know* what made him do it.

I simply don't know.

And there is no <u>Reason Four</u> because he didn't do it anyway.

Not *my* dad.

It was another dad, the lost Dad.

And he did it to another me.

Another Dawn.

The Dawn who lives in a cave.

(It's a fact, a scientific fact, that every cell in the human body is renewed over a period of seven years. Every single cell. Which means that the thing I am now is a completely different thing to the thing I was seven years ago. And although the thing I am now is only two-sevenths different to the thing I was *two* years ago, that's still enough of a difference to make me a different me.

And that's a fact.

A scientific fact.)

Of course, I know that I'm lying to myself about all this, and I know that when Mum came to me a couple of days after that cold December night and asked me (with fear in her eyes) if everything was OK . . . I know that I lied to her too.

'Yeah,' I told her. 'Everything's fine.'

'Are you absolutely sure?' she asked me. 'I mean, if there's anything, *any*thing, you want to talk to me about . . .'

But there wasn't.

There isn't.

How could there be?

*(and i feel that i'm dying
and i'm dying)*

I'm lying, but it's true: there is no <u>Reason Four</u>.

save me

Taylor and Mel are gone when I wake up. I don't know what time it is . . . it's early morning, late at night. I don't know. I can't focus my eyes properly, I can't make out the digital numbers on my alarm clock. They seem to be floating in the darkness, like fuzzy red glow-in-the-dark miniature spaceships. So I don't *know* what time it is, but it feels like that nothing time, that emptiness in the dead of night when the world is at its coldest and darkest and there is no sound anywhere.

And I feel . . .

Unholy.

I feel so sick and unholy.

God, I feel sick.

I'm lying on my bed, on top of the duvet, and all I'm wearing is the stupid pink T-shirt, and because of that I'm frozen stiff, and the stupid make-up on my stupid face is cold and mucky-stiff too. I feel like a dead thing. And I wish I *was* dead. Because at least if I was dead I wouldn't feel so gut-churningly sick.

Christ, it's un*bear*able.

My belly is cramped, my bladder painfully full. My mouth

155

is dry, my lips stuck together. I ache everywhere. I smell bad. My head is throbbing and spinning and whirling and blurring . . .

And I can't remember . . .

What happened?

What happened with Taylor and Mel?

When did they leave?

When did I fall asleep?

Why do I feel like this?

What happened?

Slowly, very slowly, I ease myself up into a sitting position. Stabbing pains shoot through the back of my head, and for a moment I think I'm going to throw up. But I manage to keep it down.

I turn on the bedside lamp, wincing at the agonizing glare of the light, and I gaze around the room. It's a mess. Bottles, cigarette ends, discarded clothes, empty carrier bags. And it stinks too. Cigarette smoke, booze, puke . . .

'Shit,' I whisper to myself, leaning down to look at the floor.

And there it is – a small pool of thin yellowy vomit on the carpet next to the bed.

The sight of it makes me gag, and as I sit here retching, trying not to be sick (while at the same time trying to remember if it was actually *me* who was sick . . . trying to picture it, then trying *not* to picture it, because the image of me being sick just makes me feel even sicker) . . . that's when I hear the sound of Jesus whining in his basket.

I look over at him.

His tail wags faintly – *timp, timp, timp* – knocking against the side of his basket, and I know it's a worried wag. It's a wag that says – *I remember when I was sick on the floor and you told me off and I know there's sick on the floor now because I can smell it and I don't want to be told off again.* I glance over at Mary's basket. She seems a lot calmer about everything – eyes half closed, the tip of her tail flicking lazily from side to side.

I look back at Jesus.

'It's all right, Jesus,' I tell him. 'It's all right...'

And that's when I remember.

Taylor's voice.

It's just talking. That's all. We're just talking.

And I remember the rain beating down outside, and the music playing (*the beat of your heart, your cold empty heart*) and Taylor asking me questions.

Was he up to something?

Who?

Your dad – was he up to something?

And now my eyes are closed and my spine is cold and I'm remembering shimmers of memories – vague thoughts about Dad, a cold December night...

I don't think God made him do it.

It was another dad, another Dawn...

Another time...

Everything's fine...

And I feel that I'm dying.

Because I can't remember if these memories are memories from inside my head, memories of thoughts, memories of dreams... or if they're memories of something I said. Did I tell Taylor and Mel about Dad? Did I tell them about that hymn-haunted night, that one time, that black hell, that cave-inducing shame . . .? I don't know. I can't think. It's all in shimmering pieces . . . *I'm not here I'm not listening . . . Who? . . . I'm not saying anything . . . God help me . . . I'm out of my mind . . . Your dad . . . I'm out of his body and soul and I'm not listening . . . Your dad – was he up to something? . . . No no no no no . . .*

I can't remember.

But I think I *might* have said something.

Something about Dad.

Was he up to something?

Up to something?

Yeah, you know . . . up to something.

Like what?

You tell me.

'Shit,' I hear myself whisper now. 'The money.'

I jump off the bed too quickly, resulting in:

(1) a sudden lurching pain in my head

(2) a dizzying whirl that rocks the floor up and down and makes me stagger to one side

and (3) a cold sticky feeling on the bare sole of my left foot as I step into the forgotten pool of vomit.

'Shit,' I mutter again, hopping around on one foot now, vainly trying to shake the sick off the other one.

And my head is still throbbing and everything around me is still spinning and whirling and blurring, and now Jesus and Mary have jumped out of their baskets and are scurrying around at my hopping feet like a couple of demented otters, yipping and yapping in delight at this unexpected (but very welcome) dead-of-night game.

'No,' I tell them, whispering loudly. 'No, *that's enough. I'm not playing...*'

It's useless though. They won't stop playing until I stop playing, and there's no point trying to keep my foot off the floor now anyway, because Jesus and Mary have both been trampling in and out of the sick, so now there's eight little doggy feet spreading it around all over the carpet...

I stop hopping and stand still.

And I wait for a second or two.

Until Jesus and Mary realize that the game is over, and they stop running around and just stand there, panting quietly, looking up at me.

And I tell them firmly, 'No more. OK? That's enough.'

They look at me.

really?

And I say, 'Yeah, really.'

well, OK... if you say so

I glance down at my foot. It's not too sicky, just a little bit gooey and yellowy at the side. I wipe it (guiltily) on the carpet, promising myself to clean it up later, then I cross my room, put on my dressing gown, open the door, and tiptoe hurriedly along the landing to Mum's bedroom.

something's wrong (2)

Mum's bedroom door is open, the room inside dark, but not fully dark. The curtains are open, letting in a rain-mottled orangey glow from the street lights outside. I can see that Mum's bed is empty. Unslept in. But that's not unusual. She quite often falls asleep in the armchair downstairs.

The house is quiet.

And cold.

My heart is dead.

The bare floorboards creak slightly as I cross over to the bed and crouch down beside the worn red rug on the floor. The rug doesn't look as if it's been disturbed. I carefully fold it back. The floorboard underneath doesn't look as if it's been moved. I hook my finger into the knothole and slowly ease the floorboard up.

The dark-green holdall is still there.

I breathe out quietly.

Then I lean down and unzip it.

It's all still there. The stacks and stacks of £20 and £50 notes, the loose £230, the matt-black automatic pistol . . . it's all still there. Which means I can't have told Taylor and Mel about it, because if I had, I'm pretty sure that either some of it or all of it wouldn't be there any more.

Which is a relief...

But not much of one.

Because if I didn't tell Taylor and Mel about Dad's money... what *did* I tell them about?

Maybe, I'm thinking (as I put the floorboard back and cover it up with the rug), maybe I didn't tell them anything. Not about Dad, anyway. Maybe I'm just misremembering it all, getting it all mixed up... confusing my thoughts and my dreams and my other-Dawn memories with the things that happened when I wasn't myself...

And why *wasn't* I myself?

And I think I know... but I don't want to think about it.

Downstairs, in the front room, the air is thick with the smell of stale cigarette smoke, the sweet stink of cannabis and the sour fruitiness of drunken breath. Mum is snoring quietly in the armchair with a burned-out cigarette dangling from her fingers. The TV is flickering mutely in front of her, its too-bright light strobing on and off in the darkness, lighting up her passed-out figure with flashes of unreal colour. I stand there for a moment, gazing at the TV screen (it's tuned to Paramount Comedy, an episode of *Everybody Loves Raymond*, the one where Robert and Raymond have a fight in their car), and then I reach down and take the dead cigarette out of Mum's fingers, drop it in the (overflowing) ashtray, and give her shoulder a gentle shake.

'Mum?' I say softly. 'Come on, Mum, wake up...'

She shudders a bit and makes a wet snorting sound, but she doesn't wake up.

I shake her again, a bit more firmly. 'Come on, Mum. You can't stay here all night . . .'

And this time she half opens her eyes, blinks in confusion, shakes her head, and noisily clears her throat. 'Whuh . . .?' she mutters.

'It's all right,' I tell her. 'It's only me.'

'Dawn?'

'Yeah.'

'Time is it?' she mumbles.

'I don't know . . . it's late.'

She's trying to sit up straight now, sleepily looking around as if she doesn't know where she is.

'You fell asleep in your chair,' I tell her.

'Sleep . . .?' she says.

'Yeah.' I hold out my hand to her. 'Come on, let's get you upstairs.'

She reaches out for my hand but misses it, grabbing hold of the sleeve of my dressing gown instead. And then, for a moment or two, she freezes, sitting perfectly still, her drunken eyes staring intently at the fold of white cloth gripped in her fingers.

'Clean . . .' she murmurs, her voice almost inaudible.

'What?'

'Clean . . .'

'I don't know what you mean, Mum. What's clean?'

She doesn't answer me. She just carries on staring at my sleeve for a second or two, then she loosens her grip, delicately brushes my wrist with her fingertips, and slowly looks up at me.

'Are you sure everything's OK?' she says distantly. 'I mean, if there's anything, *any*thing, you want to talk to me about . . .'

I look back at her, not knowing what to say.

She smiles sadly at me.

I don't think she knows what she's talking about.

'I'm tired,' she says emptily. 'What time is it?'

I help her out of the chair and take her upstairs to bed.

these days (2)

Sleep.

I don't write anything in my notebook tonight, this morning . . . there are no words to write.

I'm incapable.

Sick and scared.

Out of my mind, out of my body and soul . . . I lie on my bed and stare at a dim square of nightlight in the window, trying to stem the sickening swirl of blackness in my head.

Sleep.

about you (2)

When I finally wake up after a long and restless sleep, I still feel sicker than hell. My mouth is bone dry, my throat feels shitty, my head is thick and throbbing. My nose is blocked up, my eyes are glued shut. My room stinks. Worst of all, though, my heart is weighed down with an overwhelming sense of guilt and shame. And I don't know why. And my childish head keeps telling me that it's not *fair* to feel so guilty and ashamed when I don't even know what I've done to deserve it.

But I'm not a child.

I know that *fair* doesn't come into it.

I put my hands over my eyes.

Open my eyes.

And slowly take my hands away.

(i can see)

The curtains are open, and I can see that the only good thing about this dull January day is that it's not the middle of the night any more. The cold's not so cold, the darkness has gone (replaced by a rainy grey dimness), and the loneliness of last night's dead-of-night silence has been broken by the dreary little sounds of the day: cars, a distant siren, a front door slamming somewhere up the street. I can hear Mum too. Downstairs, clinking around in the kitchen. Making coffee, probably.

I look at my alarm clock.

It's 12.30 p.m.

Time to get up, I suppose.

About an hour or so later, after I've finally got out of bed and gone to the bathroom and scrubbed all the make-up off my face and taken a shower and washed my hair (with a shampoo that's got guarana in it, which *doesn't* give me an instant energy surge or transform the way I feel), and after I've brushed my teeth and retched into the sink a couple of times . . . I still feel terrible. And if I could be bothered to hate Taylor and Mel for doing whatever they did to me last night to make me feel like this, I would. But I can't. I can't be bothered. I really can't be bothered with anything any more. Nothing seems worth it.

Like brushing my hair.

Drying it.

Looking in the mirror.

Getting dressed.

Or killing God.

I mean, what's the point?

I can't kill God, can I? I was never going to be able to. It was an utterly pointless and futile exercise. A complete waste of time, just like everything else – painting letters on snails, wearing Invisible Coats, trying to pretend that everything's OK when nothing is ever OK . . .

Who am I trying to kid?

No, I can't be bothered with anything any more. I can't be bothered with God or games or stupid little lies. And I can't be bothered with brushing my hair or drying it or getting dressed either, so right now (after I've showered and brushed my teeth and everything, which I'm already wishing I hadn't bothered with), I just flop back into my dressing gown and slump out of the bathroom with a head full of damp knotty hair.

Who cares?

Mum, surprisingly, is sitting in the kitchen for a change. Drinking coffee (without any whisky?) and nibbling a biscuit.

'All right, love?' she says to me as I come in.

'Yeah . . .'

'I've fed the dogs for you.'

'Thanks . . . did you give them their Bonios?'

She nods, sipping coffee. 'Are you sure you're OK? You look a bit sickly.'

I sit down at the kitchen table. 'I'm fine,' I tell her. 'I just didn't get much sleep, that's all.'

'Do you want something to eat?'

'No, thanks.'

We both look down then as Jesus and Mary come trotting in through the dog flap in the door.

'Hey,' I say to them.

They come over and snuggle down at my feet. I scratch their heads. Mary farts quietly. Jesus gives her a puzzled look.

'Nice,' I say. 'Very ladylike.'

Mum smiles and lights a cigarette. She looks tired and

worn-out – her skin kind of greying and pale, her eyes a bit hollow-looking . . . but it's no worse than usual. She never looks that great any more. And I wish . . .

I wish I could stop wishing for things that aren't going to happen.

'What time are you going?' I ask her.

'Sorry?'

'Your doctor's appointment – what time are you leaving?'

She shrugs. 'About four thirty, I suppose.'

'Maybe it'd be best if you don't have a drink before you go,' I suggest.

She smiles. 'OK.'

But I know she will.

'Mum,' I say tentatively. 'Do you remember what you said last night?'

'When?'

'When I woke you up . . . you were asleep in the armchair and I woke you up. Remember?'

'Yeah . . .'

'And you said something about something being clean.'

'Clean?'

'Yeah . . . I think you might have meant my dressing gown.'

She hesitates for a moment, her eyes suddenly anxious. 'Your dressing gown?'

'Yeah.'

She puffs nervously on her cigarette and glances at my dressing gown. 'What . . . that one, you mean?'

'Yeah.'

'The one you're wearing?'

'Yeah.'

She takes another drag on her cigarette and shakes her head. 'I don't know . . . did you ask me to wash it for you or something?'

'No.'

She's avoiding my eyes now, trying to appear casually puzzled. But I don't think there's anything casual about her. She's tense, nervy . . . and I could be wrong, but she seems almost fearful about something.

'Mum?' I say softly. 'What did you mean . . . about the dressing gown?'

She tries to smile at me. 'I'm sorry, love. I really can't remember –'

'Please, Mum,' I beg her. 'Please just tell me . . .'

The doorbell rings.

The dogs jump up and start yapping.

And I can tell from the thank-God-it's-over look in Mum's eyes that there's no point in trying to ignore the doorbell.

The moment has gone.

I've lost it again.

I get up and answer the door.

It's Mel, and she's on her own. No Taylor this time. Just Mel. Which makes me feel kind of weird. Firstly, because I wasn't really expecting to see either of them for a while. I don't know why. I just sort of assumed, for no particular reason, that they'd finished with me. They'd had their fun, they'd played with their pet fat girl for a while, and now they'd want to play with something else. The second reason I feel kind of weird is that while Mel's all dressed up and made up as usual, I'm standing here in the doorway wearing nothing but a ratty old dressing gown. And all at once I'm a bit re-bothered that my hair probably looks like an incontinent crow's nest. And thirdly, I've got so used to seeing Mel with Taylor that it's just kind of unsettling to see her on her own. You know, it's like seeing Ant without Dec or something. It just doesn't *feel* right.

'Hey, Mel,' I say, tightening the belt on my dressing gown. 'Where's Taylor?'

Mel just nods at me. 'Could I come in for a few minutes? I need to talk to you about something.'

So here we are again – me and Mel, alone in my room (apart from the ever-present Jesus and Mary, of course, who are both settled down nicely in their baskets . . . and the other ever-present Jesus and Mary (Chain) too, who right now are singing the sad sweet melody of 'About You', the song I've had in my head since I woke up)

> *(there's something warm*
> *there's something warm*
> *there's something warm*
> *in everything)*

and I'm sitting at my desk (hoping that Mel can't smell the faint whiff of sick from the (almost) dried-up mess on the floor behind her (which I've forgotten to clean up)) and Mel is perched, kind of rigidly, on the edge of the bed, looking kind of . . . I don't know. Worried, maybe? Uncertain about something?

'Are you all right?' I ask her.

She crosses her legs, fiddles with her hair. 'Yeah . . .'

'Where's Taylor?'

She shrugs dismissively. 'How should I know? We don't go *every*where together, you know. I mean, it's not like she's my . . .' She pauses, looking a bit agitated.

'Sorry,' I say. 'I didn't mean anything. I was just . . .'

'Yeah, I know,' she sighs. 'It's all right . . .' She sighs again, then she uncrosses her legs, cocks her head to one side, and looks over at me with a smile. 'This is really nice . . . this music.'

'Yeah.'

> *(i know there's something good*
> *about you*
> *about you)*

'Is it that band you were talking about the other night?' Mel asks.

'Yeah, The Jesus and Mary Chain. Do you really like it?'

'Yeah, it's good.' She smiles. 'Maybe I'll get some.'

'I can lend you some CDs if you want.'

She nods, still smiling, and I think she's being genuine, she really does like the music, but I can already see her smile beginning to fade, and she's nervously licking her lips, and I've got the feeling that I'm about to find out what she's doing here.

'Listen, Dawn,' she says.

Listen.

'About last night . . .'

happy when it rains (3)

I can hear Mel's words echoing around in my head
about last night . . .
about last night . . .
about last night . . .
and I don't say anything.
I can't say anything.
I just look at her.
'Do you remember much about it?' she says eventually.
'Enough,' I tell her, my voice instinctively cold.
She lowers her eyes. 'Look, I'm not proud of what we did, OK? And I feel kind of shitty about it now. But I'm not going to pretend that I was forced into it or anything. It was just as much my idea as Taylor's.'
'You mean getting me drunk?'
She looks at me, slightly surprised.
'I'm not stupid,' I tell her. 'I mean, I didn't know at the time what you were doing . . . not at first anyway. And by the time you'd *got* me drunk . . . well, I was too drunk by then to know what was happening. But when I woke up in the middle of the night feeling sicker than I've ever felt before, it wasn't *that* hard to guess what had happened.'
'Yeah, well,' Mel mutters. 'I'm sorry . . .'

'What did you do?' I ask her. 'Did you spike the Revolver?'

'Later on, yeah . . . Taylor put a load of vodka in it. But the thing is, it's got vodka in it anyway.'

'What – Revolver?'

'Yeah, it's like one of those pre-mixed drinks, you know . . . like Bacardi Breezer and Vodka Kick and stuff. That's why we scratched the label off, so you couldn't see what was in it.'

I'm looking at her now, my eyes fixed steadily on hers, and I realize that I'm feeling surprisingly calm about everything. Whatever bad feelings I have – resentment, anger, a sense of betrayal – they're not really *true* feelings. They're just the kind of feelings you get when you think you're *expected* to feel a certain way, and although you *don't* feel that way, there's something inside you that feels the need to show that you do.

'Why did you do it?' I ask Mel.

'What – get you drunk?'

'Yeah . . . and all the other stuff too. The clothes and the make-up and everything. Pretending to like me. I mean, I know you probably thought it was funny –'

'No,' she says firmly. 'It wasn't that.'

'Yeah, right,' I say (and I can't help sounding pretty sarcastic here). 'I suppose you were just trying make me *feel better* about myself, were you?'

Mel shakes her head. 'Honestly, Dawn . . . it wasn't like that. It was just . . .'

'Just what?'

She looks at me for a few moments then, her face so serious and her eyes so troubled that I can't help feeling just a little bit sorry for her. And it suddenly strikes me that here I am, Pathetic Dawn, and the girl over there, the girl I'm feeling sorry for, is Mel Monroe. I mean ... she's *Mel Monroe*, for Christ's sake. She's hard, she's hot, she's the bad girl who all the other bad girls look up to. She can ruin your life just by looking at you the wrong way. And it was only a few days ago (or maybe it was a few thousand years ago?) that I'd seen her coming out of Accessorize with Taylor, and I'd felt so alien to them, so *unbelonging*, that I'd kept my head down and kept on going, pretending not to see them, pretending to be lost in the music ... but now here she is, Mel Monroe, bad-assed and beautiful, sitting nervously on the edge of my bed in my room. And I'm actually feeling a little bit sorry for her. And that, in turn (and unbelievably), makes me feel that I have some kind of *power* over her.

I know that I don't, of course.

I know that this is just a temporary blip in the balance of nature. And Mel knows it too. Which is why she's looking at me now, then gazing down at the floor, taking a deep breath, pulling herself together ... and finally she raises her head and looks over at me and makes herself say what she's come here to say.

'It was just for the money.'

'Sorry?'

'The money ... it was all about the money. It still is. That's why I'm here.'

'What money?'

'Your dad's money.'

When I don't say anything to that, she just stares intently at me for a moment or two, trying to work out what my silence means, and I try to keep my eyes as blank as possible. Which isn't easy, because my heart's pumping pretty hard right now, and I can feel all kinds of stuff stirring inside me.

'Look,' Mel says, 'I don't know if there *is* any money or not, and to be honest I really don't care any more. But, in a way, it doesn't *matter* if there is any money or not. I mean, if Taylor's dad thinks there is –'

'Taylor's dad?'

'Yeah. If *he* thinks –'

'Hold on,' I say, suddenly confused. 'What's Taylor's dad got to do with anything?'

Mel raises her eyebrows. 'Don't you know?'

'Know what?'

She looks at me, perplexed. 'You *really* don't know?'

I shake my head. 'I haven't got a clue what you're talking about.'

'Lee Harding,' she says. 'Taylor's dad. You've never heard of him?'

'No.'

She sighs. 'Didn't your dad ever mention him?'

'*My* dad?'

'Yeah, they know each other. Well, they *used* to know each other . . .' She pauses for a moment to light a cigarette, and all I can do is sit here and watch her, waiting, breathing, not knowing what to think about anything. 'Lee Harding,' she says, through a mouthful of smoke, 'got out of prison two or three weeks ago. He served two and a half years of a five-year sentence for ABH and dealing. That's how your dad knew him.'

'From prison?'

'No, I mean through the drugs. Lee was a supplier, a

dealer. I think your dad first met him when he was buying gear for himself, but then he started working for Lee now and then.' She looks at me. 'You do *know* that your dad was involved in all that kind of stuff, don't you?'

'Yeah.'

'He knew a lot of people, apparently. Had a lot of contacts.'

'Yeah.'

'Anyway,' Mel goes on, 'it turns out that a couple of years ago Lee was working on some kind of really big deal, something to do with a big shipment of smack, and your dad was helping him out with the distribution. You know, like selling it on for Lee for a percentage of the take . . . and then, all of a sudden, Lee gets busted, doesn't he? And the police know *exactly* where to look for the evidence they need for a conviction. And your dad's just collected on a deal worth over £200,000. The thing is, though . . . he's sold the gear and he's got the cash, but he hasn't paid anything over to Lee.'

'Are you trying to say that my dad stole Lee's money *and* grassed him up?'

'I'm not *trying* to say anything. I'm just telling you what I've heard.' She looks at me. 'I mean, think about it. Your dad's got more than 200 grand that belongs to Lee Harding –'

'Yeah, OK, but if Lee was in custody by then, how was my dad *supposed* to pay him?'

Mel shakes her head. 'He'd already had the cash for a week or so *before* Lee was arrested. And, anyway, it doesn't work like that. There were other people involved, they had a system . . . your dad didn't have to hand over the money to Lee directly. He could have got it to him if he'd wanted

176

to. And then, once Lee's been banged up, your dad goes and disappears . . . and no one's seen him for the last two years . . . so, you know . . .' Mel looks at me. 'It all kind of adds up, doesn't it?'

'You think so?'

She shrugs. 'It doesn't matter what I think. All that matters is what Lee Harding thinks. And he thinks your dad took his money and tipped off the police.'

'And now Lee's out of prison.'

'Yeah . . . and he wants his money back.'

I stare at her, trying to think things through, trying to work out if what she's saying makes any sense. 'But why has he waited until now?' I ask her. 'I mean, I know he was in prison, but you said that there were other people involved . . . why didn't he just get some of them to go looking for his money?'

Mel takes another drag on her cigarette. 'Lee's a bit of a psycho. He likes to deal with this kind of thing *personally*, if you know what I mean.' She looks into my eyes. 'So, you know . . . if you *do* know anything about the money −'

'Wait a minute,' I say. 'How do *you* know about all this?'

'I told you, he's Taylor's dad . . .'

'So?'

She sighs (like, does it *matter* how I know?). 'Look,' she says, 'we were at Taylor's place, OK? A few weeks ago . . . sometime before Christmas. And we happened to overhear her dad talking to some of his friends. They were all stoned, you know . . . Lee had just got out of prison and they were throwing this kind of welcome-home party for him. Anyway, we heard them going on about this guy called John Bundy −'

'Oh, right,' I say, interrupting her. 'And I suppose Taylor just happened to mention that she goes to school with his daughter?'

Mel shakes her head. 'No . . . Taylor didn't know you were his daughter. Not then, anyway. She's pretty new at school, don't forget. I mean, she knew you were called Bundy, but she didn't know anything else about you. As far as she was concerned, you were just that weird girl from school who never spoke to anyone –'

'The fat todger-dodger with no friends?'

Mel smiles. 'Yeah.'

'But *now* she knows who I am.'

Mel nods. 'She asked me . . . you know, she asked me if you were related to this John Bundy guy, and I told her –'

'You *knew* he was my dad?'

'Not for sure, no . . . but I'd heard about your dad going missing, and there were all these rumours about him doing drugs and going to prison and everything, so I just kind of guessed it was probably the same guy. I mean, there aren't that many people called Bundy around, are there?'

I shrug.

'So, anyway,' Mel goes on, 'after we'd heard Taylor's dad and his friends talking about your dad, Taylor and me decided to check you out. You know, we thought we'd find out for sure if you really were John Bundy's daughter, and then we'd just kind of poke around a bit, see if you knew anything about the money.' Mel stubs out her cigarette. 'Taylor reckoned that if we got the money back, her dad might let us have some of it.'

'Right,' I say. 'So all this . . . the two of you coming round here and making out like you're friends of mine, and all that crap with the clothes and the make-up and getting me drunk and everything . . . it was all just for the money?'

'Yeah. Listen, I'm sorry –'

'Did you look for it?'

'What?'

'The money. I mean, after I'd passed out last night . . . did you look for it?'

'Yeah . . . well, Taylor did. But she didn't find anything.'

'And I suppose she asked me where it was when I was drunk, did she?'

'Yeah.'

'But I didn't say anything?'

Mel hesitates. 'Not about the money, no.'

And now I'm hesitating too. 'What do you mean?'

She lights another cigarette. 'Do you remember Taylor asking you about your dad?'

'Yeah, vaguely.'

Mel shakes her head, blowing out smoke. 'She was trying to be all clever about it. You know, she was trying to find out if you knew anything about the money without letting on that that's what she was doing. Do you know what I mean? It's like she couldn't just come straight out and ask you about it, she had to try and be clever. *What was he like, your dad? What do you remember about him? Was he up to something?*' She shakes her head again. 'I *told* her to just *ask* you about the money. You were too drunk. It wasn't fair . . .'

I look at her. 'What wasn't fair?'

She closes her eyes for a moment and sighs. 'You were too drunk . . . you just started rambling. And it was really hard to understand what you were saying. It was like you were having a nightmare or something, you know ... just blurting out all this stuff that didn't seem to make sense.'

'What kind of stuff?' I ask quietly.

Mel holds my gaze. 'Stuff about your dad.'

I don't know how I feel now. There's an emptiness in my stomach, a remembrance of pain. A suffocating blockage in my throat. And deep inside the darkness of my cave I can feel a tingle of tears in my eyes. But the tears are too far away to come out.

I can't speak.

My eyes ask the questions.

And Mel answers. 'You kept saying "it wasn't him",' she tells me. '"It was someone else ..."' She stares at the ceiling, concentrating, trying to remember. 'And there was something about *prayers* ... and something else about *washing* something, I think. And *blood*.' She looks at me. 'The blood of something?' She puffs thoughtfully on her cigarette. 'And you kept trying to say "stop him" ... but it was like you couldn't say it properly, or you kept getting it mixed up or something. It sounded like you were saying "stop *the* him ..."'

'Hymn,' I mutter, staring at the floor. 'Stop the *hymn* ...'

'What?'

I look up at Mel. 'Nothing ... it's nothing. I'm sorry ... I can't ...'

'It's all right,' she says softly. 'I understand.'

'Do you?'

'Yeah, I think so. That's partly why I'm here.'

I give her a puzzled look. 'What do you mean?'

She sighs. 'It made sense to me.'

'What did?'

'The stuff you were saying last night, when you were drunk... the stuff about your dad. I know I just said that it *didn't* make sense, and it didn't in a way... you know, it wasn't like you were giving anything away. I mean, Taylor didn't have a clue what you were talking about.'

'But you did?'

She nods soberly. 'I think so.'

I look at her, waiting for her to explain.

After a few seconds' silence, she says (very quietly), 'I had a brother... Oliver...'

She pauses then, staring blindly at the floor... and I remember her doing exactly the same thing when she mentioned her brother before. She'd not said anything else about him then, she'd just whispered 'my brother' and sat there in silence, as if she was totally alone. This time, though, she doesn't look quite so lonely, and I get the feeling that she's going to tell me more.

I sit very still and wait.

After another few moments, she closes her eyes, swallows hard, then breathes out shakily and goes on. 'Oliver was thirteen at the time. I was about ten... he was my big brother, you know? He used to look after me.' She smiles sadly to herself at the memory. 'He used to go to this local youth club thing, you know, one of those places that's supposed to help kids with problems... not that Oliver *had* any problems. I mean, he'd just got himself into a bit of trouble nicking cars and stuff... that's all it was. Anyway, there was this vicar...

he used to come round to the club now and then to talk to the kids about . . . I don't know. I suppose he talked to them about fucking *morality* and shit . . .' Mel's voice is gripped with bitterness now. 'I don't know how it happened,' she continues, 'but somehow Oliver got mixed up with this vicar, and they started having these *special* little talks together, you know, on their *own* . . . and then . . . shit, I don't know. I was only ten, for Christ's sake. I didn't know what was going on. And, of course, my mum and dad didn't know how to deal with it, so they wouldn't tell me anything . . . I don't really know exactly what happened even now.' She takes another deep breath. 'All I know is that Oliver killed himself, hanged himself, and he left a note behind for Mum and Dad telling them how sorry he was, how ashamed . . . and then there was all this stuff with the police and the vicar and everything . . . Christ . . .'

Her voice trails off as she wipes a tear from her eye.

'Shit,' I whisper.

She nods.

'What happened to him?' I ask. 'The vicar, I mean.'

She shakes her head. 'Nothing . . . fucking *nothing*. He denied it all, didn't he? Said it was all in Oliver's mind. And there was no proof . . .' She shrugs. 'He got moved away, that's all. The vicar. They moved him to another town somewhere.' She stares at nothing for a moment, lost in her thoughts, then she puts out her cigarette and looks over at me. 'We used to share a bedroom,' she says. 'Oliver and me. He used to have nightmares sometimes, you know, when all this stuff with the vicar was going on. He'd talk in his sleep. It didn't make any sense to me at the time . . .' She pauses, looking thoughtfully at me, asking me if I understand.

I nod at her. 'Some things are too hard to talk about.'

'Yeah ... but you can still understand them.'

I nod again. 'Yeah ...'

And then, as we sit there for a moment or two, letting the (Jesus-and-Mary-Chained) silence hang in the air, there's a quiet knock on the door and we both look round as it inches open and Mum's head appears (as if floating) in the gap.

'I'm off to the doctor's now, love,' she says.

'Oh, right,' I say, glancing at the clock (16:32). 'I didn't realize it was so late ...'

Mum smiles nervously at Mel. 'Hello ...'

'Hi,' says Mel, smiling back at her.

'Right, well,' Mum says awkwardly, turning to me again. 'I'd better get a move on or I'll be late ...'

Her eyes are filmed with a slight sheen of drunkenness.

'Are you all right, Mum?' I ask her.

'I'm fine.' She smiles at me. 'I'll see you later, love. OK?'

'Yeah, OK. Bye ...'

Her smile is already fading as her head retreats and the door closes behind her. I listen to her footsteps shuffling slowly down the stairs. I hear her pick up her keys and open the front door ... a pause ... then the door slams shut.

'Is she always like that?' Mel asks me.

'What – nervous?'

'No, drunk.'

My instinctive reaction is to deny it, but when I gaze over at Mel and see the knowing look in her eyes, I realize there's no point.

'Well, she's not *always* drunk,' I tell her.

'But more often than not?'

'Yeah . . . pretty much.'

Mel nods. 'Mine's the same.'

'Really? Your mum?'

'Yeah . . . she was always a *bit* of a drinker, but after Oliver killed himself . . . well, it all got too much for her. Dad too. They couldn't cope with it. They split up about a year after it happened. Mum's been drinking herself to death ever since.' Mel lights a cigarette and smiles at me. 'Life, eh?'

'Yeah, I suppose . . .'

'You're meant to say *it's a bitch*.'

'Am I?'

'Yeah.'

'OK . . . it's a bitch.'

She laughs then, and it sounds good. It sounds tired and hopeless too – in a got-to-laugh-or-else-you'll-cry kind of way – but it still sounds good.

'So, anyway,' she says, her laughter dying with a weary sigh. 'Do you get it now? I mean, do you see what I mean about understanding?'

'Yeah . . . (*I can see that you and me live our lives in the pouring rain*) yeah, I think I get it. Well, most of it, anyway.'

'Which bit don't you get?'

I shrug. 'Why you're here. I mean, I'm not saying I don't appreciate it or anything, and I realize it must have been really hard for you –'

'It's not *hard* for me.'

'I didn't mean –'

'Don't fucking *patronize* me, Dawn.'

'I wasn't –'

'Look,' she says, tight-lipped, 'I didn't come round here to tell you all this because I feel *sorry* for you or anything . . . OK? Because I don't . . . and I don't want you to feel sorry for me either. D'you understand?'

'Yeah.'

'I mean, I know what you're going through . . . that's all. I know what it's like. And I just wanted you to know . . .'

'Why?'

'*Why?*'

'Yeah, why did you want me to know?'

'Because . . .' She shakes her head. 'Shit, I don't know.' She bows her head, breathes in deeply, then blows out her cheeks (like she's finally decided to tell the truth) and looks over at me. 'All right,' she says quietly. 'I like you, OK? I think you're . . . you know . . . I think you're all right. And I just wanted to let you know . . .' She hesitates, looking troubled.

'It's all right,' I tell her. 'You don't have to –'

'Yeah, I do.'

'I know what you're trying to say.'

'No, you don't.'

'All right,' I say, slightly impatiently. 'So *tell* me then.'

'It's Taylor's dad,' she says simply, her eyes fixed on mine. 'Lee Harding . . . he's coming round here tonight.'

almost gold

After last night, Mel tells me, after they'd got me drunk and
Taylor had tried (and failed) to get me to tell her about Dad's
money (or maybe I should say Lee Harding's money?), and
after I'd passed out and Taylor had had another look round
the house and not found any obvious hiding places . . . after
all that, on their way home, Mel tells me, Taylor had told
her that she was going to tell her dad about me.

'I tried to persuade her not to,' Mel says, 'but she'd already
made up her mind. The way she saw it, her dad was going
to find out where you live sooner or later anyway, and Taylor
reckoned that if he found out from her, she might still be in
line for a cut of the cash.'

'So she told him?'

'Yeah. I rang her this morning. She said she told him last
night. She told him everything. You know, about us coming
round here and checking you out, about your mum being
drunk all the time, about all the expensive stuff you've got . . .'
Mel looks at me. 'He's coming round tonight, Dawn. From
what Taylor told me, he thinks you've either got the money
somewhere here, or you're still in touch with your dad. He's
coming round here to find out.'

'When?'

'About seven thirty, Taylor reckons.'

I look at the clock (17:11).

'I'm sorry,' Mel says. 'If I'd known –'

'Do you think he'll come on his own?' I ask her.

'I don't know . . . probably. I mean, he knows there's only you and your mum here, so it's not like he needs any protection or anything. And, like I said, he likes to deal with this kind of stuff personally.' She looks at me, her eyes deadly serious. 'He's not a nice guy, Dawn. He's not nice at all.'

I'm trying to think about things now. I'm *trying* to think about what it all means and what's going to happen and what, if anything, I can do about it . . . but it's all so ridiculous, so ludicrous, so head-spinningly unreal . . . it's impossible to even *begin* thinking about it. All I *can* think about right now is – how the hell did I get from my world of nothing to this?

Q. How do you get from a world of perfectly contented loser-ness, a world of Nothing Coats and dogs and snails and letters and songs and useless ideas about killing God . . . how do you get from there to here? How do you get to be sitting in your room on a rainy Thursday afternoon with a beautiful mystery-girl sitting on your bed telling you stuff that's too unreal to comprehend?

A. I don't know.

'Listen, Dawn,' Mel says (and I look up from my stupid reverie to see her getting up off the bed and crossing the room towards me). 'Are you OK?' she asks, stopping in front of me.

I smile at her. 'Not really.'

She puts her hand on my shoulder and she looks me in the eye and says, 'Look, I know I'm probably the last person in the world you want any advice from, but if I were you ... well, I wouldn't try to hide anything from Lee Harding. I mean, if you *do* know anything about the money, it might be best to just tell him.'

'Yeah?'

'Yeah.'

'Best for who?' I ask, staring right back at her.

She doesn't say anything for a moment, she just looks at me, and I know she knows that I'm suddenly beginning to doubt her seemingly good intentions. I don't *want* to doubt her, and I definitely don't *like* the idea that she's still playing games with me, but there's a part of me that can't help thinking that maybe all this apparent concern of hers – the confessions, the sharing, the stuff about liking me – maybe it's all just another way of getting me to tell her what she really wants to know: i.e. where's the money?

She takes her hand off my shoulder and steps back, a look of disappointment in her eyes. 'I'd better go,' she says quietly.

'You can't blame me for not trusting you,' I tell her.

She smiles at me. 'I know ... I don't blame you. I'm just trying to ...' She shakes her head and starts doing up her coat. 'It doesn't matter. There's nothing I can say, is there? I can't *make* you believe me.'

I watch her as she zips her coat. 'You don't have to go.'

'Yeah, I do.'

I carry on watching her. 'What about Taylor?'

'What about her?'

'I don't know . . . I just . . .'

I don't know what to say.

Mel looks at me. 'It's just how I cope, OK?'

'What do you mean?'

'Taylor, being with her . . . being the way I am.' She shrugs. 'I mean, all this fucking hard-ass shit – it's the only way I know. It's what I have to do to be all right. Just like you have to do what you have to do to be all right. Taylor's just a part of it, that's all.'

'Yeah, but you spend all your time with her. You must *like* her.'

She laughs. 'Liking's got nothing to do with it. She's either my friend or my enemy, that's all there is to it. And she's too much of a bitch to have as an enemy.'

'The easiest way out . . .' I mutter.

'Yeah, exactly.'

I smile at her. 'So I don't suppose there's any chance of *us* being friends, is there? Even though you think I'm all right.'

Mel grins. 'No chance. I've got a reputation to keep up.'

'But you *do* think I'm OK?'

She moves closer to me. 'Yeah . . . I said so, didn't I? I think you're OK.'

'And you like me.'

'Yeah . . . I like you.'

'But when you see me at school, you still won't talk to me.'

She shakes her head. 'You're Dawn Bundy. If I start hanging around with you, I won't be Mel Monroe any more. I need to be what I am.'

'Yeah, but maybe –'

'No maybes, Dawn,' she says, putting her hand on my shoulder again. 'It's not going to happen.' As I look up at her, she puts her other hand on my other shoulder and leans in close to me. 'Sorry,' she whispers. 'But that's just how it is.'

And then she kisses me, perfectly, on the lips.

And we look into each other's eyes for a moment.

And Mel smiles.

And that's it.

'I have to go,' she says, stepping back.

I start to get up, my legs a little wobbly.

'It's all right,' she tells me. 'I'll see myself out.'

I pause, looking at her.

'What's the matter?' she smiles. 'Don't you trust me?'

I hesitate for a second – torn between wanting to see her out, but not wanting her to think that I don't trust her – and then I lower myself back into the chair.

'Yeah,' I tell her. 'I trust you.'

She smiles again. 'OK . . . well, I'll see you . . .'

'Yeah.'

She opens the door. 'And don't forget what I told you.'

'I won't.'

And with that, she's gone.

I listen to her footsteps skipping lightly down the stairs.

I hear her open the front door . . . a pause . . . (and I'm already lost now, lost in my head, lost in the memories of what just happened . . . the taste of her kiss . . . and the things I wish I could make never happen).

I'm already lost.

never saw it coming

It's five thirty now. And if Mel was right about Lee Harding, that means there's only two hours to go before a seriously unpleasant man comes hammering at my front door.

One hundred and twenty minutes.

It's not a lot of time.

And I know that I shouldn't be wasting it by lying here on my bed, still in my dressing gown, with my eyes closed and my dogs lying (on their backs) beside me and my iPod on full volume and my head full of music and words and memories of kisses and hymns and dead brothers and caves and vicars and fathers and mothers and daughters . . .

No, I shouldn't be thinking about these things.

But I am.

Q. Why?

A. Because I've already thought all there is to think about Lee Harding, and all I've come up with is a list full of can'ts:

    1) I can't call the police because they'll want to know why Lee Harding is coming round here, and I can't tell

them about the money because it's drug money and Dad stole it.

2) I can't get in touch with Dad because I don't where he is, or even if he's still alive. And even if I could get in touch with him . . .

3) I can't think about that.

4) I can't call Mum because she doesn't have a mobile phone.

5) I can't just leave the house and hide away somewhere until Lee Harding has been and gone because:

(a) he'll only come back again later

and (b) Mum's going to be back soon (actually, she should be back already, but I'm not surprised that she's not. I expect she's stopped off in a pub on the way home for a drink or two, or three or four). But, anyway, she'll be back soon, and I can't leave her to deal with Lee Harding on her own.

6) I can't *do* anything, can I? All I can do is lie here, lost in my music and memories, and wait for Mum to come home. And hope that she isn't too drunk. And then . . .? What's going to happen then? I don't know. We'll talk, I suppose. I'll tell her what Mel told me. And we'll try to work out what to do.

Maybe we'll decide to give Lee Harding the money.

Or not.

Maybe we'll lie to him.

Or maybe not.

Maybe we'll both be too scared to do anything.

And he'll just shout at us.

Or beat us up.

Or worse . . .

I don't know.

All I can do right now is lie here, listening, and hope that nothing will happen.

nine million rainy days (1)

I'm half asleep when it happens. I'm still on my bed, still in my dressing gown (with my eyes still closed and my dogs still lying (on their backs) beside me and my iPod still playing), and I'm in that wonderful twilight place that bridges the world between sleep and non-sleep, the place where you can dream without dreaming and sense without knowing. Your senses are closed, your mind is in darkness. Your body is there and not there. You can hear without listening. You can hear the sounds inside your head and you can hear the sounds outside your head, and you don't know which is which. The sound of a thought becomes the sound of a song. The sound of a song becomes a picture of things you can't see. And the music in your head becomes whatever you want it to be.

(nine million rainy days
have swept across my eyes
thinking of you
and this room becomes a shrine
thinking of you)

Your life.

(and the way you are)

Your ghost.

(sends the shivers to my head)

And then something moves. And just for a moment you think

(you're going to fall
you're going to fall down dead)

you're dreaming. You think (in your half-sleep) that the movement you felt is not a movement but a sound, or the feeling of a sound . . . but a split second later, when you feel it again, you know that you're wrong.

You're not dreaming.

You're awake now.

Wide awake . . .

And you're instinctively aware that the movement you felt was Jesus, that you were resting your hand on his body (feeling his dog-heart beating in time to the music) and that the first movement you felt must have been the sudden tensing of his muscles, and that the second movement you felt must have been when he jumped off the bed (with Mary) and started barking like mad at the bedroom door (*ROW-ROWROWROWROWROWROW*).

Which they're both still doing now.

Which means there's someone in the house.

And now you're not just awake, you're *hyper*-awake, ripping out your earphones and sitting up straight and listening hard . . . breathing hard, listening hard . . . but all you can hear is the frenzied yapping of your dogs. And you know that they wouldn't be barking like that at your mum, so now you're glancing desperately at the clock, hoping (please) that it's not seven thirty yet . . .

And it's not.

It's five past six.

So Lee Harding *shouldn't* be here yet . . . but then the dogs stop barking for a second, and you hear a muffled footstep on the stairs – a careful step, a creak, a pause – and time doesn't matter any more.

You're petrified.

Staring rigidly at the door.

Your arms crossed tightly.

Clutching your dressing gown to your chest.

And . . . *Jesus Christ.*

The door is opening.

The door is *opening*.

And the dogs have gone silent, backing away.

And you've stopped breathing.

This isn't real, it can't be . . .

But it is.

It's real.

The door is open.

And a man is standing there, looking at you.

'Hello, Dawn,' he says.

nine million rainy days (2)

I can see him, standing there in the doorway, his tattered figure haloed in the dusty light... I can *see* him. His washed-out eyes looking at me. His face unshaven, pale and drawn. His once-blond hair now raggedy brown, matted and darkened with rain...

I can see him.

My dad.

I can't speak.

'Can I come in?' he asks nervously.

I can't speak.

'Dawn?' he says.

'Dad...?' I breathe.

He smiles anxiously. 'I'm sorry... I didn't mean to frighten you. I just...' He glances over his shoulder. 'The front door was open... I thought...'

'Mel...' I mutter.

'Sorry?'

'Nothing... a friend of mine was here, that's all. She must have left the door open when she went...' I stare at him. 'God, I can't believe it's you...'

He shrugs. 'It's me...'

'What are you doing here?'

'We need to talk, Dawn,' he says. 'And there's not much time . . . do you think I could come in?' He lowers his eyes. 'It's all right if you don't want me to . . . I mean, I understand. I can stay here if you want . . . or if you want me to go –'

'No, it's OK,' I say quietly.

He looks at me. 'Are you sure?'

I nod.

As he steps cautiously into the room, Jesus and Mary (with equal caution) waddle up to him with their heads held low and their tails wagging warily. It's a tail-wag that says – *are you* really *who we think you are?*

'Hello, dogs,' Dad says to them.

Their tails wag faster.

Dad looks at me. 'Is it all right if I sit over here?' he asks, gesturing at my desk.

'Yeah.'

I'm not really sure how (or what) I'm feeling as I watch him move over to the desk and sit down. Empty, I suppose . . . I just feel empty. Blank. Too shocked to feel anything. And maybe that's for the best, because there's too much I *could* be feeling right now – fear, anger, hatred, disgust . . . embarrassment, shame, despair, disbelief . . .

> *(and all my time in hell*
> *is spent with you)*

It's all too much.

Jesus and Mary have jumped back on the bed now, and Dad's sitting down at my desk. He looks so different to how

I remember him. He looks old, worn out, beaten down. He looks dull – dull eyes, dull hair, dull clothes. He looks like a man who buys his clothes from the dull-old-man-clothes section in charity shops. He also looks unfamiliarly sober.

He smiles tentatively at me. 'You're still listening to The Jesus and Mary Chain then?'

I look down at my iPod on the bed beside me. It's still playing, the tinny-sounding music still audible through the earphones.

(i have ached for you
i have nothing left to give
for you to take)

I don't want to talk about music.

'Where have you been all this time, Dad?' I ask him, my voice a lot colder than I mean it to be.

He looks sadly at me. 'I'm sorry, love . . . I didn't want it to be like this. I didn't want to just turn up out of the blue –'

'Where have you been?' I repeat.

He shakes his head. 'Nowhere really . . . I've got a little flat on the other side of town, across the river. You know the St Thomas estate?'

'The big tower blocks?'

He nods. 'It's OK . . . a bit noisy sometimes, but you know . . .' He glances distractedly around the room, then looks back at me. 'I've got a job too,' he says. 'You know . . . a real job. Nine-to-five and all that . . . well, not quite nine-to-five.' He grins, embarrassed. 'I deliver furniture.'

'Furniture?'

'Yeah . . . it's not the most exciting –'

'Farthings,' I say suddenly. 'Farthings Furniture . . . it's your van, isn't it? The blue one.'

He doesn't say anything for a moment, he just lowers his eyes again and absentmindedly picks at his nails. And as I look at him, I realize that there's something else about him now that wasn't there before: a complete lack of vitality. He has no energy. No zest. No life. I mean, before, when he was still My Dad, he'd never sit as lifelessly as he's sitting now. No matter how drunk or stoned or whatever he was, he'd be fidgeting all the time, constantly changing position, his eyes never still. But now . . . well, now he's just sitting there, all hunched up, almost motionless. Like there's nothing left of him. Or nothing left *for* him.

'You've been watching us, haven't you?' I say to him. 'In your van . . . you've been watching me and Mum.'

He looks up at me. 'I just wanted to . . . I don't know. I just wanted to make sure you were OK, that's all. I wasn't *spying* on you or anything . . . I was just . . . I just wanted to *see* you. You and your mum . . . I couldn't bear it, not seeing you.'

'*You* couldn't bear it?' I say angrily. 'What about *us*? How do you think *we've* been feeling?'

'I'm sorry –'

'Not knowing where you are, or even if you're still alive . . . I mean, Christ, Dad – we didn't know *any*thing.'

'I didn't think –'

'You could at least have let us know you weren't dead. You know, a phone call, a letter . . .'

'I *am* dead,' he says blankly.

'What?'

'I wanted to be dead. I didn't want to live any more. Not after . . . you know. Not after that. But I couldn't . . . I couldn't do it. I couldn't make you hate me even more.' He lowers his eyes. 'And killing myself wouldn't have been enough anyway. It wouldn't have changed anything. So I made myself live with it . . . every day . . . with nothing to take the pain away . . . and that's killed me more than dying ever could.'

'You're not drinking any more?' I ask quietly.

He shakes his head. 'Not since I left. Nothing . . . no booze, no drugs . . .'

'What about God?'

'No,' he says, swallowing hard. 'No God. There never was . . .'

'What do you mean?'

He sighs. 'It was all just me, Dawn. Me . . . whatever I was, whatever I am . . . it was never anything to do with anything else. All that God stuff was just . . . I don't know. It was just another excuse, you know . . . just something . . . somewhere to hide . . .' He sighs again, wiping at his eye. 'I didn't know what I was doing, Dawn. I didn't know . . . I mean, I don't even know . . .'

'What?' I say sharply. 'You don't even know what?'

He breathes out heavily. 'I'm sorry . . . I can't . . . it's too late. I can't make it better.'

'So why are you here then?' I snap at him. 'What do you want, Dad? Do you want me to forgive you?'

'I could never ask you to forgive me.'

'Yeah, well,' I say nastily. 'Maybe you should try it.'

'I don't deserve –'

'I'm not talking about what you deserve!' I scream at him.

'I'm talking about *me*! Me, Dad. *ME!* What do you think *I* deserve? I mean, you asked your precious *God* for forgiveness, didn't you? You fucking asked *him*.'

Dad's just staring at me now, his empty eyes struck with confusion and fear. And I can't be angry with him any more. I *want* to . . . I want to let him know how I feel, I want him to understand me. I want him to understand what I want from him. But he just doesn't get it. He doesn't understand. And I don't know if that's because he's sick, dead, deluded, disturbed, fucked up by a lifetime of drugs . . .

I just don't know.

And I don't know if it makes any difference either.

You can only be what you are.

I can't hate him.

(i have no more empty heart
or limbs to break)

'Just tell me what you want, Dad,' I sigh. 'Why are you here?'

'To warn you,' he says, glancing at the clock.

'Warn me about what?'

'A man called Lee Harding.'

He starts telling me all about the money then, how he stole it from Lee Harding and tipped off the police, how he left us the money when he disappeared because he didn't want Mum to have to worry about getting a job, how he realizes now that he was in such a state at the time ('completely and utterly fucked up', as he puts it) that he didn't know *what* he was doing . . . and I'm so confused about everything at first – getting Mel's story mixed up with Dad's story . . . then and now, now and then – I'm so tangled up inside my head that I don't do anything. I just sit there, speechless, dumbly letting Dad carry on with his story.

'I just didn't think,' he tells me. 'It never even occurred to me that I might be putting you and your mum in danger.' He shakes his head, dismayed with himself. 'I suppose I thought that Lee would be put away for a lot longer –'

'So that's the *real* reason you're here, is it?' I say, surprised at the venom in my voice. 'You're worried about your money.'

'No . . . I told you. I came here to warn you –'

'Yeah, well, that's really good of you, Dad. Really thoughtful. Thanks a lot.'

He frowns at me. 'I don't understand –'

'No, I don't suppose you do,' I say, glaring at him. 'I mean, you think it's all right to come strolling back into our lives just because some tough guy's coming round here to get his money back . . . you think *that's* all right. But what about Mum and me? What about all the shit and pain that we've been going through for the last two years? You don't think *that's* worth coming back for?'

'But that's different –'

'No, it's not, Dad.'

He looks at me, wanting to say something, wanting to explain why it's different, why he couldn't come back before . . . but he just can't do it. And I think I want to tell him that he doesn't have to explain, that I know it's different, but I just can't do it either.

So I just kind of breathe out, letting it all go, and I say, 'I know all about Lee Harding.'

'Sorry?'

'I know all about it – Lee Harding, the money . . . everything.'

'You *know*?'

I nod. 'Mel told me. Mel Monroe, the girl I mentioned earlier. She's friends with Lee Harding's daughter, Taylor.'

'Right . . .' Dad says thoughtfully. 'And this Mel . . . she told you all about Lee Harding?'

'Yeah.'

'Everything?'

'Yeah.'

'Did she tell you he's coming round here tonight?'

'Yeah.' I look at the clock. 'In about an hour. That's what you wanted to warn me about, isn't it?'

He nods, looking confused. 'Why did she tell you about Lee Harding?'

'Because . . . well, it's a long story.' I look at Dad. 'How do *you* know he's coming here?'

'It's a long story,' he says, trying a smile.

I don't smile back, I just stare at him, demanding an answer.

His smile fades and he lets out a long and weary sigh. 'When I found out that Harding was getting out of prison, I knew it wouldn't be long before he started looking for me, and I was worried that he might try to find me through you and your mum. Or worse, he might find out that you've got his money. So, basically, for the last few weeks or so I've been keeping a close eye on everyone – Harding, his friends, his family, you and your mum . . .'

'So you know about Taylor and Mel coming to see me?'

'Yeah . . .'

'Did you know who they were, what they were doing?'

'Not at first. I just thought they were friends of yours. But there was something about Taylor, you know . . . something vaguely familiar about her, like I'd seen her somewhere before or something. So when they left here the other night, I followed her home. And that's when I realized who she was.' He shrugs. 'I still didn't really *recognize* her, but I suppose I must have seen her at Lee's place a couple of years ago . . . and, you know . . .'

'You put two and two together . . .?'

He shakes his head. 'Not really. All I knew then was that Lee Harding's daughter had just spent a couple of hours with my daughter. I mean, I kind of guessed that *some*thing was going on, but I didn't know what it was.' He looks at me, his eyes uncertain.

'Don't worry, Dad,' I say (kind of sneerily). 'I didn't tell her anything about the money.'

'I know you didn't,' he says matter-of-factly. He looks down at his hands again. 'Not that it would have mattered if you had . . .' And then, after a moment's thoughtful silence, he looks back at me. 'I followed Taylor again last night . . . or this morning . . . whenever it was she left here. I waited outside Lee Harding's house all night. And I've been following him around all day. That's how I know about him coming round here . . . I heard him talking about it with some of his friends in a pub.'

'You followed him into a pub? Weren't you afraid he might see you?'

With an embarrassed smile, Dad digs into his pocket and

206

pulls out a pair of glasses and a baseball cap. He puts them on. 'It's pretty pathetic, I know, but it seems to work. And anyway . . .' He takes off the hat and glasses. 'I mean look at me, Dawn. Do I *look* like me any more?'

(and the way you are
sends the shivers to my head)

'What are we going to do, Dad?' I ask him.

'About Lee Harding, you mean?'

'Yeah.'

He looks at the clock (18:45).

'Have you still got the gun?' he asks me.

'The gun?'

'The one I left with the money.'

'Yeah . . . we've still got it.' I look at him. 'Is it yours?'

'Does it matter?'

I don't say anything, I just keep staring at him.

He sighs again. 'It was just . . . it was just something I had, that's all. For protection. I never used it –'

'Why did you leave it here?'

'I don't know. I didn't *mean* to leave it . . . it was just in the bag with the money . . .' He glances at the clock again, then looks back at me. 'Where is it, Dawn?'

'Why? What are you thinking of doing?'

'Listen,' he says. 'I really don't care about the money, OK? Harding can have the money. And he can do whatever he wants with me too . . . but not here. This is between me and him. No one else. If he so much as *looks* at you or your mum . . .'

'What?' I say. 'You'll shoot him?'

Dad looks at me for a while then, not saying anything, and I get the feeling that he wants to tell me that he's just trying to do what he thinks is right, but he doesn't want me to think that he's trying to put *every*thing right, because he knows that he can't.

And I have absolutely no idea what I'm feeling.

One second this, the next second that . . .

You're my dad.

You're a monster.

I hate you.

I loved you.

I love you.

How can I love you?

How can you be my dad?

(as far as i can see
there is nothing left of me)

You killed me.

For God's sake.

You made me. You unmade me.

You put me in a cave and left me there to die.

(and all my time in hell
was spent with you)

You *are* my dad.

'Dawn,' he says now, very quietly.

I look at him. 'What?'

'Your mum'll be back soon. We need to –'

'She went to the doctor's,' I say emptily.

'I know.'

'You followed her?'

He nods. 'She left the surgery around half past five and went for a drink.' He glances at the clock. 'She left the pub about half an hour ago. She should be home any minute.' He hesitates, looking awkwardly at me. 'Is she . . .? I mean, is she all right?'

I shrug. 'It was just a routine appointment –'

'No, I mean generally . . . you know . . . how is she?'

'How do you think?'

He nods sadly. 'Is she drinking a lot?'

'Yeah.'

'Does she . . .?'

'Does she what?'

He shakes his head. 'Nothing . . . it doesn't matter . . .'

I look at him, sitting in his silence, and I can see that he loathes himself. And I can see that he knows there's nothing he can do about it. There's nothing he can feel to make things right – shame, guilt, regret, remorse . . . they're all just useless emotions.

They don't change anything.

Nothing changes anything.

I look down at my iPod, the distant song still playing

(nine million rainy days
have swept across my eyes
thinking of you)

209

and I turn it off.

I get up off the bed.

Dad looks over at me.

I glance down as Jesus and Mary hop off the bed and go trotting out of the room (and the part of me that's still connected to the real world realizes that they haven't been out for a wee for a while, so that's probably where they're going), and then I look back at Dad.

'I can't say anything,' I tell him quietly.

'I know,' he says.

My eyes are tingling now, and I know that I really *can't* say anything. All I can do is what I'm doing. And as I move slowly towards Dad, I don't know if what I'm doing is right or wrong, or why I'm doing it, or even what it means . . . I don't know anything.

I'm just moving.

Walking towards him . . .

Stopping in front of him . . .

Looking into his eyes.

All I want to do is hold him for a moment. That's all. Or have him hold me. I just want us to be what we were again – me and my dad – just for a moment . . .

My arms move.

I reach out awkwardly for Dad's head.

He leans slowly towards me.

I take his head in my arms.

He tenses, keeping his body away from me, but he lets himself be held.

And then I move a little closer . . .

Hold him a little tighter.

And, very cautiously, he moves to hold me back.

And then . . . I don't know how it happens. Maybe I jump a little as his hand touches my arm, or maybe his hand just brushes against the sleeve of my dressing gown and catches in the cloth . . . I don't know. But suddenly I'm aware that my dressing gown has come open at the front, and just for a moment I can feel Dad's stubbly cheek resting against my naked skin . . . and I *know* it's an accident, I know that Dad's already realized what's happened and has quickly moved his head away . . . *I* know that it's *not* happening again. But the other me doesn't. The other me – the Cave Dawn, the thirteen-year-old Dawn – all she's ever known is the pain of that moment and the terror of living it again, and now she thinks that she *is* living it again. And she panics.

She cries out, a yelp of fear, and pushes Dad away . . .

She steps back, too quickly, almost losing her balance as her hands grab desperately at her dressing gown, trying to cover herself up . . .

And then – *BANG!*

The world suddenly explodes.

And I look on in horror as Dad grunts, a godless sigh, and slumps to one side in the chair.

drop

The room is heavy with silence now. The sudden *BANG!* has stopped ringing in my ears, the air is still, and I can see everything as it always will be. I can see my father, slumped to one side in the chair, blood oozing slowly from a bullet hole in his chest. I can see him, breathing painfully. I can see flecks of pink spit bubbling on his lips.

I can see that he's dying.

I can't speak.

'Dawn?' a frail voice says from the doorway.

Mum.

I can see her. She's standing there with Dad's gun in her hand, her ashen face wet with tears.

'Are you all right?' she asks me.

I nod.

'Did he hurt you?'

I shake my head.

'You're bleeding,' she says numbly, gazing at my legs.

I look down at myself. The whiteness of my dressing gown is spattered with blood, some of which has smeared on my legs.

It's not mine.

It's Dad's.

I look at him. His eyes are wide open, staring wildly. His chest rattles and he coughs weakly, bringing up blood. His face is white.

He opens his mouth, trying to say something.

'. . . *uhh . . . uh . . .*'

He coughs up blood again.

I fall to my knees in front of him. 'Dad . . .?'

His eyes struggle to focus on me.

'. . . *Dawn . . .?*' he whispers.

'Dad . . .' I sob, choking back tears. 'It's all right, Dad . . . you're going to be OK . . . it's all right . . .'

'. . . *please . . .*'

And I can see him dying now. I can *see* it happening . . . right in front of me. I can see the light fading from his eyes.

'No, Dad,' I cry. 'Don't . . . just hold on . . .'

'. . . *forgive me . . . please . . .*'

'. . . don't die . . .'

'. . . *forgive me, Dawn . . .*'

And I want to tell him that I *do* forgive him . . . I want him to *know*, right now, before it's too late . . . but I'm crying so much now . . . I can hardly breathe . . . and the words are stuck in my throat. I can't breathe . . . I can't swallow . . . I can't get the words out . . .

And then – in a moment of absolute emptiness – Dad just dies.

There's nothing to it.

He just goes limp.

His eyes switch off.

And he dies.

sundown

We're sitting on the floor, Mum and me. We're in my room, sitting on the floor, in front of Dad's body. We're holding each other, crying in each other's arms. We're drowning together. And right now I truly believe that this is the end. There can't *be* anything else. Not after this. There can't be any tomorrows, there can't be anywhere else, there can't be a moment that *isn't* right now. This room, this floor, these tears, this blood – this is all there is.

This is all that can ever be.

This is . . .

No.

Listen . . .

The rain.

This is not the end.

I can still hear the rain on the window. The rain is still falling. This is not all there is. This room, this floor . . . these tears. I can hear them becoming something else now. Something more. A voice. My mother's voice. Sobbing to me in despair.

'. . . I couldn't . . . I couldn't let him do it, love . . . I had to stop him . . . I couldn't let him . . . not again . . .'

She's crying so hard that I can barely understand what she's saying.

'It's OK, Mum,' I say, holding her tightly. 'It's OK...'

'... I didn't want to ... I didn't ...'

As I stroke her hair, letting her weep, her tear-sodden words sink slowly into my mind:

... I couldn't let him do it, love

... not again ...

... I had to stop him ...

... not again ...

And even if I didn't know it before (and I'm not sure that I didn't), I know it now: she knows what happened. She knows what Dad did to me. She's known it all along. That's why she killed him. She must have heard his voice when she came upstairs. She must have got the gun from her room, fearing the worst ... and then she'd come into my room and seen the worst: me and Dad together. She'd seen me pushing him away, my dressing gown undone. And she'd seen the terror of the other Dawn in me, and – just like the other Dawn – she'd thought it was happening again.

She couldn't let him do it.

Not again.

'How did you know, Mum?' I ask quietly.

She shudders. 'What?'

'About Dad, you know ... Dad and me ... how did you know?'

She looks at me, trembling, wiping snot and tears from her face. 'I'm *so* sorry ... I didn't ... I should have *done* something ...'

'How did you find out?'

She looks away from me, looking down, and I feel her putting her hand on my leg. I look down. She moves her hand, gently fingering the bloodstained hem of my dressing gown.

Her voice, when she speaks, is a broken whisper. 'I thought it was just you at first . . . the blood on your dressing gown . . . I thought you were just having your period. The sheets too . . . I didn't think . . .' She pauses, staring curiously as a single tear falls from her eye and drops on my leg. She reaches out and touches it with her bloodied fingertip. The teardrop turns pink. 'He was bloody . . .' she murmurs. 'He was . . . in the night . . . I saw it. And the terrible things he said . . . in his sleep . . .' She shakes her head. 'There were other things too . . . I can't tell you. But I knew. And then he left . . . I just . . . I didn't want to believe it . . . I couldn't . . .' She looks up at me, her face distraught. 'I loved him, Dawn . . . I didn't know what to do . . . I'm so sorry . . . I just didn't . . .'

'It's OK, Mum,' I say softly. 'It's all right . . .'

'No,' she sobs. 'It's *not* all right . . . how *can* it be all right? How could he do that to you? He loved you . . . how could he *do* that?'

'I don't think he knew what he was doing, Mum . . . he was too . . . I don't know. He was all messed up.'

'That's no excuse.'

'I know . . .'

She takes hold of my hand and stares hard into my eyes. 'I couldn't let him hurt you again, Dawn. You understand that, don't you?'

I look back at her, not knowing what to say. What can I

say? She's just killed the man she loves . . . she killed him because she thought she had to. She thought she was saving me. But she was wrong.

I can't tell her that, can I? It would kill her.

But if I don't tell her . . .?

If I don't tell her the truth, she'll always believe that Dad was unforgiveable. She'll never know that maybe, just maybe, there was a part of him that was still worth loving.

How can I deny her that?

And how can I deny him a chance for her forgiveness?

Forgiveness . . .

I look at him now, just slumped there, cold and dead in the chair. And I'd like to believe that there's still something there . . . something, somewhere . . . something of Dad that somehow knows what's in my heart. I'd like to believe that he can still hear me.

I forgive you, Dad.

I forgive you.

But I can't.

There *is* nothing else. This is it. This world, this life, this time – this is all there is.

Life and death.

Death . . .

It leaves things behind.

And that's what I'm thinking now, as I sit here in this room, on this floor, staring at the cold reality of my father's lifeless body – his death leaves things behind. It leaves a space where he should be. It leaves me stained with blood and tears. And it leaves my mum with murder on her hands. And that *is* the cold reality – my mum is guilty of murder.

And unless we do something about it right now, that really could mean the end.

I look at the clock (19:15).

'Mum,' I say. 'We have to do something.'

her way of praying (3)

I can't stop to think about this, I just have to do it. And there isn't much time left, so I'm having to do it quickly – getting up off the floor, helping Mum to her feet, trying to get through to her . . .

'Come on, Mum . . . we have to go.'

'Go?'

'Can you walk all right?'

'Walk?'

'Please, Mum . . . you have to go downstairs. Right now. Come on . . .'

She looks at me – trance-like now, helpless and hopeless. I don't think she knows what's happening.

'Downstairs?' she mutters.

'Yeah,' I say, ushering her towards the door. 'Wait for me in the front room.'

She doesn't say anything, she just shuffles out.

'I'll be down in a minute,' I call after her.

I turn round and scan the room.

I feel weirdly focused.

Like I know what to do without knowing.

Do it.

1) Pick up your iPod, turn it on.
2) Earphones in, select something fast.
3) Wait for the crash to kick in . . .

(fall to her call on a saturday night
she's got the hip dipping trick
of all time done right)

and 4) Pick up the gun from the floor.
5) Grab something to wipe it with (you almost smile when you realize you've picked up the bright-pink *ROCK 'N' ROLL STAR* T-shirt) and wipe the gun clean.
6) Wrap it in the T-shirt, put it in your pocket, and go.

(like a sin scraping skin)

I know that I *can't* stop to think about this, that I just have to do it, but that doesn't mean that the doubts aren't there. And as I'm hurrying into Mum's bedroom and getting the holdall out from under the floorboards, the doubts are already getting louder, screaming into my head with the music . . .

(she is screaming for me)

But this thing I'm doing, I really haven't thought about it. I haven't *created* it. It simply appeared, fully formed, inside my head: this is what you have to do.

And I don't have time to question it.

Q. Why don't you just call the police and explain what happened? Your father abused you. Your mother killed him to prevent further abuse. So, yes, she'll probably be charged with his murder (or manslaughter), and she'll probably stand trial for it too. But she'll never be convicted of anything. She saved her daughter from the most despicable crime imaginable, and no one in the world would ever blame a mother for that.

So why don't you just call the police?

A. Because if I call the police, everything that's happened will come out, and the rest of the world will think that John Bundy was evil, that Sara Bundy is weak, and that Dawn Bundy is a victim. And we will become those things.

So, as quickly as possible, this is what I have to do. I have to take the holdall and the gun downstairs (not even stopping to comfort Jesus and Mary, who are both still trembling with fright from the sound of the gunshot earlier on). I have to go to the front door and set it on the latch. I have to move back along the hallway and put the gun on the floor, about two metres away from the door. I have to move further back, three or four steps, and place the holdall on the floor. I have to open it, so the money is visible. And now I have to stand here and think for a moment, picturing how this will work.

Q. How will this work?

A. Like this:

a) Lee Harding will arrive and find the door on the latch.

b) I'll call the police.

c) Lee Harding will cautiously open the door and come in.

d) He'll see the gun and the holdall on the floor.

e) He'll see the money in the holdall.

f) He'll be confused, wary.

g) He'll look around, maybe call out, and then he'll pick up the gun.

h) And then, when the police arrive, they'll find a dead body upstairs and Lee Harding in the house with a gun in his hand . . .

i) . . . and they'll find out from me (and my mum, after I've told her what to say) that he came round here to see my dad about some stolen drug money, and they had an argument, and he shot my dad . . .

But I think I know, even now, that it's not going to work. There are too many things that could go wrong. What if the police don't show up? What if they take too long to arrive? What if Lee Harding doesn't show up? What if he does, but doesn't pick up the gun? What if he does pick up the gun but runs off when the police arrive? What if . . .?

No, it's a useless idea.

It's never going to work.

It's pathetic.

But what else can I do? It's almost seven thirty now.

It's almost time.

(and I just can't take it anyway)

All I can do is resign myself to it. Whatever's going to happen, it's going to happen. I take one last look at the gun and the holdall on the floor, shake my head, and go into the front room.

who do you love?

So here we are again, in the front room. Mum's in her armchair, watching TV, smoking a cigarette and drinking her drink. I'm on the settee, with Jesus and Mary squeezed in tightly beside me. And we all seem to be watching *World of Mysteries: Tutankhamun's Curse* on Sky Three. The curtained darkness of the room is illuminated with the flashing light of the monstrous TV, and every now and then, when the picture on the screen suddenly brightens, the TV light catches the cloud of cigarette smoke that's hanging beneath the ceiling, and just for a moment the cloud is a lightning cloud, and I'm not sitting in the front room any more, I'm sitting outside and a storm's about to break and I seem to be some kind of . . .

Something.

I'm nothing.

I've told Mum (very quickly) about Lee Harding, and I've told her that I'm going to call the police when he gets here, and I've told her what to say to them when they arrive . . . but I'm not sure how much of it she's taken in. She seemed to be listening to me, and she nodded her head whenever I asked her if she understood, but she didn't ask me any questions about anything. She just waited for me to finish, smiled at me, then turned on the TV.

'It'll be all right, Mum,' I say to her now. 'As long as we stick to our story . . .'

'Uh-huh . . .' she mutters, her eyes glued to the TV screen. 'Stick to the story . . .'

'It'll be OK.'

'OK . . .'

Her eyes are glazed, her voice is sleepy. I don't think she's here any more. She's traumatized, stunned, shocked, drunk . . . she's gone to that place where she goes to cope. She's in her cave.

It's OK.

She doesn't have to function.

I can do that for her.

She's my mum.

I love her.

nine million rainy days (3)

It's only when the doorbell rings that I finally realize (with a stupid sinking heart) that I should have got changed out of this bloodstained dressing gown, because as soon as Lee Harding sees me covered in blood, he's going to turn round and run off, isn't he? And even if he doesn't run off (and he'd have to be pretty dumb not to), I'm not going to have time to get changed before the police arrive, am I? And even if I did have time . . .

The doorbell rings again.

And I wonder for a moment why Jesus and Mary aren't making a sound. They're not barking, they're not moving, they're not doing anything. They're just sitting there, looking at me.

I look at Mum.

She doesn't do anything either.

She just carries on staring at the TV.

And I wonder for another moment why Lee Harding is ringing the doorbell when I purposely left the door on the latch . . . but somehow it doesn't seem to matter any more.

I get up.

Go out into the hallway.

Pause for a moment . . .
And open the door.

*(you're going to fall
you're going to fall down dead)*

It isn't Lee Harding.

inside me (4)

Everything stops (for ever) when I see the two policemen standing on the doorstep in front of me. Time stops, the world stops . . . nothing moves, nothing makes a sound.

The moment is frozen.

I see it as a picture, a freeze-framed picture at the end of an endless story.

(i take my time away
and I see something)

This is what I see.

First thing – a pair of uniformed policemen in fluorescent yellow jackets, standing in the rain, staring silently at me with their seen-it-all eyes.

Second thing – a frozen flash of siren-blue from the patrol car parked in the street behind them.

Third thing – the street, a rainy-grey tarmac ribbon, slicked with the sheen of petrol rainbows.

Fourth thing – the same-as-always row of houses on the other side of the street. Black windows, dirty-white walls.

One or two faceless faces are peeking out through gaps in the curtains.

Fifth thing – a car passing by, a silver BMW, its movement frozen like everything else. Taylor is in the passenger seat, looking over at me, her eyes unreadable, and I guess the man in the driving seat is her father. Lee Harding. He has a bullet-shaped head, closely cropped hair, a diamond stud in his ear. His eyes are looking straight ahead. This is nothing to do with him.

Sixth thing – across the street, half hidden behind a dirty blue van (with *Farthing's Furniture* written on the side), a ten-or-eleven-year-old boy in a rain-sodden parka standing alone on the pavement. He's smiling at me, giving me the thumbs-up. And the look in his eyes – a mixture of excitement, curiosity, approval-seeking and pride – tells me everything I need to know about this final picture.

Splodge must have called the police.

He must have seen the blue van when it arrived earlier on.

He must have seen Dad getting out of the van and going into my house, and he must have remembered me telling him (for snail-related reasons) about a non-existent man who'd parked his non-existent van outside my house the other day, a non-existent man who'd sneaked into the alleyway that leads round to my garden.

You should have called the police, Splodge had said to me.
Yeah, well, I'd told him. *If I see him again, I will.*

And Splodge must have listened to me.

(And maybe he heard the gunshot too.)

And called the police.

And here they are, standing on the doorstep in front of

me, their uniformed figures frozen in the blue-flashed rain . . .
and, any moment now, when the world starts moving (for
ever) again, their seen-it-all eyes are going to see the blood-
stains on my dressing gown.

And that's going to be it.

They're going to ask me about the blood. They're not
going to be satisfied with whatever mumbled answer I give
them. They're going to come inside, see the holdall and the
gun on the floor, call for backup . . . start searching the
house . . . they're going to find Dad's body . . .

They're going to find out that Mum killed him.

And that's going to be it.

The End.

Unless . . .

'I killed him,' I hear myself say (and at the sound of my
voice, the world starts moving again).

'You what?' says one of the policemen.

'It was me. I killed him.'

(and that's my story)

'Killed who?' the second policemen says.

'My dad.'

Before the policemen have time to react, I sense a
reassuring presence behind me, and I feel a gentle hand on
my shoulder, and I hear the sound of Mum's shaky (but firm)
voice.

'She didn't do it,' she tells the policemen. 'She didn't kill
anyone.'

I look round. 'No, Mum –'

230

'It's all right, love,' she says softly, smiling at me. 'It's over now.'

'What's going on here?' the first policeman says to Mum.

Mum looks at him, her eyes perfectly steady. 'My husband ... he's dead. I shot him. You'll find his body upstairs.'

the living end

There's a lot for me and my mum to talk about now, but as we sit here together on the settee, holding hands and crying quietly (with Jesus and Mary lying at our feet), we don't really have much time for talking. The house is full of people – policemen, detectives, ambulance men, CSIs – and they're all going about their business, and that business includes asking us questions, examining us, making sure we don't make a run for it, and pretty soon we're both going to be taken away to the police station . . . so, like I said, we don't have a lot of time for talking right now.

But, in a way, I think that's OK.

The silence between us is a good silence. We're sitting close together, we're holding hands, we're intensely aware of our love for each other – and, right now, that's all I need. Of course, we're both absolutely devastated about Dad (and we will be for the rest of our lives), and I'm worried sick about what's going to happen to Mum, and I think we both know that the next few months, the next few years, are going to be incredibly hard, especially if we end up being taken away from each other, which I think is a real (and terrifying) possibility . . .

But we're together now.

And even if we do get split up, the togetherness we have now will still be there. We're *together*.

And somehow that makes all the difference.

It makes things not quite so impossible.

When the time is right, I'll tell Mum about Dad. I'll tell her how much he hated himself for doing what he did... to both of us. And I'll tell her that he came back to help us, not to hurt me. And that he was sober. And that he still loved her very much. And I'll tell her, with my hand on my heart, that there used to be another Dawn, a thirteen-year-old Dawn, a Dawn who lived in a cave inside my head...

But she's gone now.

The other Dawn has gone.

And there's no one in my head but me.

Dawn Bundy.